WULFSTAN: AN ANGLO-SAXON THEGN

An Earls of Mercia Story

M J Porter

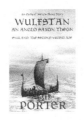

D1520012

For M Fullerton, my wonderful Gran.
'Me see, me like.'
See you on the beach.

CONTENTS

PROLOGUE - AD991

At the Battle of Maldon

From his place atop the minor rise, he watched the battle play itself out before him. More than anything he wanted to run back into the foray, his sword raised and ready, his shield in place. The impulse was instinctive.

He'd trained for this. It was his place to be, not out here, away from the heat of the battle feeling useless and unskilled.

Beneath his legs, his horse shuffled from side to side. The animal, Heard, was keen to be away from the smell of the sea and the tang of shed blood. If only he could turn away, but he knew he couldn't. He needed to watch what was about to happen so that at the least he could tell his Lord's son all about his final moments. He hoped he had a good death, a warrior's death, not pissing himself with fear when the moment came.

They'd never spoken about the final moments. They'd never been the need to before. They'd always known that they were going to emerge as the victors.

Not this time, though.

He gazed out to the vast expanse of sea, scanning the huge Viking fleet that had come to their lands, unbidden and without warning. Years it had been since the last concerted attack by the raiders. They'd come in dribs and drabs, a stray Norseman and his warriors just testing their luck and more often than not going away empty handed or with little apart from their lives, or not at all. But not in their masses. Not ninety-three ships full of bristled warriors, and rumour had it, would be kings.

He sighed deeply at the most composed attack his land had faced from across the sea throughout his adult life. He should have known that it was all too good to be true. That the small attacks would eventually coalesce into something more menacing. He fervently wished they hadn't.

These men from the north seemed less honourable than the English warriors; either that or they just saw an opportunity and exploited it. He wondered if he'd ever decipher why Ealdorman Brythnoth had decided to let the attackers cross the marshy land instead of hemming them in with the rising tide. He could accept that it was the English thing to do, to give the men a fighting chance, but it had allowed them to win the battle, or would allow them to win the battle, and he couldn't help thinking that it had been a foolish mistake. A life-ending mistake.

An honourable mistake but a mistake all the same.

The gentle smash of shields on wood touched his ears becoming muted as it travelled the great distance between him and the battle. He noted that tears were falling freely down his face. He raised his hand and wiped them angrily away. It wasn't that he felt he shouldn't cry, more that if he did cry he'd not be able to see the battle before him.

Around him, the press of the other retreating men had faded away. Now only he and a priest from Ealdorman Brythnoth's household stayed and watched, a silent vigil for dead men who yet lived.

The priest was praying quietly, and Wulfstan appreciated the soft words and the exhortations to their God that he was making. It made a strange contrast, the words of the priest, the almost silent but deadly battle before him, and the view of the gently bobbing fleet of raider ships. A beautiful tableaux and one he would have given anything not to see and not to witness.

The sails on the raiding ships were half cast down, but on the ones that still stood he could discern patterns in the weaves and wondered if they depicted who owned the vessels. If they did, he detected three separate designs or colour schemes. Did that mean three individual war leaders were facing his Lord?

He thought he might quite like his ship, but then he reconsidered, perhaps not. The sea was calm today and still they swayed haphazardly in the water, just watching them was making him feel a little ill at ease. He had no stomach for ships. He never had.

The rising voice of the priest recalled him to his gruesome task.

He squinted into the sunlight and saw what the priest saw. The defenders were slowly thinning, the attackers coming ever closer to the back of the shield wall, and when they broke through there would be no one else to stop them. Their victory would be complete. There was no one other than him and an old priest to offer any further resistance.

His Lord still stood, but barely. Somehow out of all the men, he could pinpoint where he stood without any effort. The familiar slicing action as he fought, the usual stance as he placed his weight behind the shield.

His mouth dry, his breath rasping he watched in horror as a mighty warrior, blond and bulky, cleaved his way to where Ælfwine stood. The other warriors seemed to fall away to either side of them as he focused on them.

A crash of shields, he imagined the noise although it did not reach him, and the figures were fiercely engaged in battle. He couldn't see the individual sword strokes, the rise of the war-axe; instead, he saw only the impact that the weapons had on the two men. First Ælfwine staggered and then the mighty warrior, and then once more it was Ælfwine's turn and then the other warrior's, but even from such a distance he could tell that Ælfwine was the weaker of the men, his years going against him. He was an old man, although not as old as others he knew, still, at their age, their movements were slower, and it was clear to see who'd be the victor.

And now he did turn away, slowly and with sorrow, for, after all, he didn't want to watch his Lord fall in battle. It was enough to know that he would.

His horse, keen to finally be away from the carnage, stepped lively when it was turned to face inland. It was Ælfwine's horse, and he knew it would guide him home whether he wanted to meet his son, Leofwine or not.

His son, a lad no more. His son, a Lord from now on and sure to be recognised by the King for his father's ultimate sacrifice.

An orphan at the hand of the raiders.

PART 1

CHAPTER 1 – AD978

The Witan

Wulfstan watched the Ealdorman Ælfhere carefully. He wasn't at all convinced he liked the older man, and he was certainly unhappy with the way Ælfwine was deporting himself before him.

Ælfhere carried himself with the vigour of youth amongst the assembled mass, and Wulfstan wasn't fool enough to realise it wouldn't cost him deeply to be so sprightly. He imagined that by tomorrow his muscles would have seized and he'd barely be able to take a step, let alone bound from one conversation within the great hall to another. It was all about appearance with Ælfhere and Wulfstan both admired and deplored it.

He had once brown hair, now streaked with grey and intelligent green eyes that watched everything and nothing, all at the same time. His voice was insistent and yet quiet and everyone who was his supporter treated him with great respect. Even some of those who didn't follow his policies would be offended if it were ever pointed out to them that they dipped and bowed before him, as though he were royalty.

Ælfwine was making an idiot of himself and Wulfstan was embarrassed for him. He was unused to being the focus of such a powerful man. It was evident that he didn't know how to take the shower of compliments that were being liberally pressed onto him, even when most of them were false, as he was introduced to important man after important man at the Witan.

They were within the King's Palace at Winchester, waiting for the Witan to begin. Until then Ælfhere was working hard to bend Ælfwine to his will, to have him become a firm adherent to his party, and Wulfstan was uncomfortable with it all, despite the fact that Ælfwine owed his new position as a King's Thegn to Ælfhere's efforts.

It was obvious to Wulfstan, even as unskilled as he was in the art of politics, that Ealdorman Ælfhere was up to something. The smug expression on Ælfwine's face told him his assumptions were correct, even though Ælfwine refused to speak to him about it on the few occasions he came close enough for Wulfstan to raise a quizzical eyebrow and press him for more details of just what exactly they were doing at the Witan.

They'd been summoned to the hastily convened Witan in the wake of the sudden death of the boy King, Edward. He'd barely cooled in his grave and yet already the great men and women of the kingdom were assembled at Winchester. King Edgar and his son, Edward, had been the only Kings that Wulfstan had ever known. The new King was very much an unknown for someone who'd never ventured to the Witan before, someone who until a short space of time ago had been a happily married man raising his family. Until his wife ....

He didn't like to brood on that.

Events in his home life had been just as tumultuous as those at the Witan for the last three years. He didn't like to dwell on it, but he did miss his young sons terribly.

King Edward had been a youth, fifteen at his coronation at Kingston upon Thames and eighteen at his death. His rule had been short and chaotic in places, and a tragedy had befallen the entire Witan earlier that year when the upper floor of the palace had collapsed at Calne, crushing people to death underneath the weight of those on top. Even now the men and women working their way through the great hall cast suspicious glances upwards as though daring the second story to fall down on them.

Wulfstan had heard that men and women skilled in wood-craft had been called to inspect all the King's Palaces in the wake of the tragedy. He believed the truth that it had been an unfortunate accident and nothing more sinister. It hadn't been God's judgment on the boy's reign despite those who said it had been in whispered outrage.

Still, it had shocked and sobered everyone, and Wulfstan had hoped that some sanity would prevail amongst the men and women who vied for power and control over Edward, a youth still too nonsensical and driven by his wants and desires, to think of England as a whole. Edward had been volatile and prone to violent outbursts. Wulfstan from his home in Mercia had worried that he'd not prove to be a good king, unable to control the two great ealdormen, Ælfhere and Æthelwine. Now he was even more concerned at the rumours surrounding his sudden and tragic death, and the actions of both Ælfhere and Æthelwine needed scrutiny.

It didn't help that Ælfwine owed his elevation to the Ealdor-man of Mercia, Ælfhere. An old and tested man of politics made an ealdorman in the reign of King Eadwig over twenty years ago and able to hold his position ever since. Even through the division of England once more into Wessex and Mercia under the feuding brother kings, Eadwig and Edgar, Ælfhere had managed to remain loyal to the true king and had kept his position when England had been reunited once more on the premature death of young Eadwig.

Ælfhere was entrenched at the Witan and completely caught up in the intrigue that ran through it. In fact, Wulfstan was convinced most of the conflict could be laid firmly at his feet. His, and Ealdorman Æthelwine's, and probably the Queen's as well.

Ælfhere's name was a part of the malicious rumours flooding the land, and Wulfstan, even as naïve he was, couldn't help thinking that Ælfwine's new position owed too much to the old man. He was trying to bolster his supporters at the Witan now that he was so powerful and close to the boy king. It was that, rather than any genuine belief in Ælfwine's ability to govern in the name of the king, to serve as his king's thegn and representative, that drove Ælfhere's relentless actions.

King Edgar, Æthelred's father, had calmed the often-calamitous Witan as men had grown powerful in their spheres of influence, and his long reign had proved the balancing act between the factionalism of the Court. Sadly with his unexpected death, and the three short years his eldest son had ruled, everything appeared to be regressing. Wulfstan wasn't keen on politics, but he knew enough never to be relaxed in the hall they were meeting within and he watched his every step and every word, taking the time to see who supported whom, and to drink only sparingly, just one of the hundreds called to make this momentous decision.

When the members of the Witan were called to order, all of the Ealdormen ponderously taking their seats at the front of the hall, directly before the dais, he sat on a hard wooden stool, within the vast hall, at the very rear of the assembly. He watched, and he stayed silent. He was but a tiny element of the Witan, only allowed inside because he was his Lord's senior advisor, his commended man.

At his side, Ælfwine had been bolstered by Ælfhere's blatant attempts to include him within his circle of cohorts and that concerned Wulfstan. Ælfwine might well be a grown man, able to make his decisions, but his head seemed to have been turned by the great Ælfhere and his family.

The small boy, Æthelred, now King in all but name, finally showed himself in the great hall, walking sedately through the assembled mass of men and women, looking as regal as a ten-year-old child could, escorted by a slight girl. She was somewhat his elder, but not by much. Wulfstan watched them, feeling old and out of place. The two surviving children of King Edgar shared their father's appearance. Æthelred's long blond curls escaping from behind his ears and flashing across his eyes in the slight breeze of his passing.

As Wulfstan watched him, he knew a moment of remorse for his sons and Æthelred both. He couldn't imagine his sons being able to act so calmly and self-assured in front of so many people, some smiling with joy and others with black faces, dismay at this turn of events easy to see. He couldn't imagine that Æthelred wasn't aware of the rift running through the Witan, even as young as was.

Wulfstan flicked his gaze to those the young King walked towards. The King's mother was nervous and assured all at the same time as she hovered, almost out of sight, on the dais Æthelred walked toward, her rich gown enough to feed a few hundred people throughout the winter.

Wulfstan could see, even now, why King Edgar had married the woman and made her his consecrated queen, the first of England. He could understand why, if the rumours were true, their marriage had been built on passion and desire. She was beautiful and beguiling. Her clothing immaculate and well made, if simple, but the jewels she wore at her throat, on the brooches of her dress, and threaded through her long hair, belied the wealth she had at her fingertips.

If a Viking warrior happened to stride into the room and did nothing more than pluck the jewels from her hair, he'd live a long and happy life with men to command and reward handsomely.

Wulfstan swallowed against the grief in his throat for his sons and focused on maintaining the reticence that was needed to survive in the Witan. The two powerful groups of people who dominated, on one side the young King and his mother, on the other those who'd been fervent supporters of the dead King Edward, were not about to allow either party any leeway.

Wulfstan wondered how a small youth was supposed to hold his own amongst so much pent up aggression? How could he keep order, keep men within the required boundaries of acceptability, and yet move the men forward to a mutually agreeable resolution all at the same time? How was he to accomplish the work of men when he was a boy?

A hushed silence had fallen, but as Æthelred seated himself on his father's royal dais, on a chair that was too high, his legs too short to allow his feet to touch the floor, a murmur of resentment started to build at the sight of such a slight creature.

Now was the time for the men and women to discuss the future, and the ancient Archbishop of Canterbury, Dunstan, stumbled his way up the dais, and then rambled through his welcome.

Wulfstan kept his eyes downcast. Dunstan was fiercely respected by many, but it was clear to Wulfstan that the best of his days were behind him. Only when the first to speak for young Æthelred stood on the dais, did Wulfstan glance up again.

He didn't recognize the man, but others seemed to, and quickly he realized that this was Æthelred's Uncle, the Queen's brother. He knew, even before the man opened his mouth to speak, that he'd support Æthelred. And he was proved right. Ordulf, for that was the man's name, spoke of Æthelred's ancestry and then proclaimed him support for him.

Wulfstan was unsure why the man was allowed to speak, but again, he overheard another conversation and understood. Ordulf had been an ealdorman, but King Edward had replaced him when King Edgar died. No doubt Ordulf would be keen to regain his position when his nephew ruled.

Still, his proclamation was met with resounding cheers, especially from a young man on the same row as Wulfstan.

"Who's that?" he whispered to Ælfhere under the sound of the cheers, but Ælfhere shook his head, unsure himself.

The next to speak was a holy man, his robes trailing behind him as he replaced Ordulf on the dais. This time Ælfhere leaned into his ear.

"Bishop Ælfric. This should be interesting."

The name meant little to Wulfstan, but the man spoke well, against Æthelred, and then added the words that had long been rumoured.

"Good people of the Witan," the Bishop said, a glint of triumph in his eyes. "I would speak against the young Æthelred. He can't be king when his own mother killed our previous king."

A commotion greeted those words, and Wulfstan grimaced.

He had no time for such games, for that was what the bishop was playing. At his side, Ælfwine sat with a grin on his face, enjoying the spectacle. Wulfstan shook his head, once more disappointed in his Lord.

Yet, the smile faded quickly. It wasn't that men and women were horrified by the accusation, rather they were outraged that such an allegation could be levied at the Queen. Wulfstan found his interest piqued, and turned to Ælfhere.

"Did you know?" Wulfstan hissed at Ælfwine, wondering why he spoke so quietly when the great hall had erupted in outrage. It had become obvious to Wulfstan that Ælfric was somehow in collusion with Ealdorman Ælfhere.

"He didn't say as much." Ælfwine tried to counter, but Wulfstan pressed the point, for he had heard both the rumour about the Queen, and also another, about Ealdorman Ælfhere himself.

"Do you think there's truth in the rumours that he killed Edward?"

Ælfwine hushed him in shock, his face showing a moment of panic.

"No I don't, but even if there was, we're a part of his entourage now, we can't speak against him."

Wulfstan wasn't best pleased with that announcement. He could already tell that just by allying themselves with Ealdorman Ælfhere, they were putting themselves in an untenable position.

"I wish you'd told me of Ælfhere's intentions?" he said heatedly, and Ælfwine turned blazing eyes his way.

"I'm not going to tell you everything," he hissed through his teeth, and Wulfstan felt his temper rising.

The jumped up little prick was going to get them all killed at this rate.

"You either speak to me truthfully and about everything or I don't serve you."

Ælfwine raised a contemptuous eyebrow at him.

"Where will you go then?"

Wulfstan pointedly turned to stare at the doorway to the

hall. It was opened in an enticing way, and the thought of just slipping out was overwhelming. But Ælfwine was right. He'd made his oath to him, and he had nowhere else to go, not now. Not with his wife .... All he had was his honour, and it was that which kept him in his seat, instead focusing back on events within the hall.

The general hubbub had died down as drinks were shared amongst the two hundred odd strong Witan, by servants in matching tunics, showing the emblem of the dragon of Wessex, and then another of the ealdormen took his place on the dais.

Wulfstan recognized the man. Ealdorman Æthelmær. He'd been one of King Edward's supporters, or so rumour had it. And indeed, as he spoke Wulfstan could tell the man was genuinely sorrowful for the early death of Edward. No matter the actual circumstances, someone had committed regicide, and there was a horror of such an action in the eyes of many. The few ealdormen might tirade about who would be king next, but some still lingered on who had been king, and the fact that he was dead.

Ealdorman Æthelmær surprised Wulfstan by offering his support to the young Æthelred, while Ælfwine fidgeted next to him. It seemed that Ælfwine still knew more than he'd shared with Wulfstan. That infuriated him, and he wasn't surprised when Ealdorman Ælfhere was the next to speak.

Wulfstan had thought the man an ally of the Queen, but as he paused, to show his grief for the boy who he might have just played a hand in murdering, Ælfhere showed too keen an interest and that intrigued Wulfstan.

Sure enough, Ealdorman Ælfhere soon had the entire Witan enraptured as he spoke of the longevity of the House of Wessex. However, his next words were a shock. Wulfstan, for once, admired the Ealdorman's political prowess, his ability to lull everyone into thinking one thing, before announcing the exact opposite.

"I think it's long over time that we members of the Witan concluded that the kingdom of England will never be strong enough to survive while we rely on the blood of King Alfred, who was himself a usurper of the kingdom of Wessex. His family are not the rightful rulers of England. Not when we have another, here in this very room, who should wear the crown of England and govern her as she should be governed."

"Ealdorman Æthelweard stems from ancient bloodstock, just as old as this upstart branch of the House of Wessex. His line can be traced back to the beginning of Wessex because he's a relative of young atheling Æthelred. And what's more, he is a man grown, with his own family, and children who will rule after him."

Ealdorman Ælfhere spoke as though the matter was resolved, and beside him Ælfwine jiggled his legs with excitement, but Wulfstan was unsure. What had caused this change? Why, when Ealdorman Ælfhere's name was almost synonymous with the Queen's, had he chosen to support another?

Wulfstan glanced at Ælfwine. What game had he been enticed into playing?

But Ealdorman Ælfhere hasn't finished speaking.

"What would we rather? A child king now, or an adult king with children who will grow to maturity in the coming years? Would we rather wait for this child to grow before he can father children, or would we rather have a man who has proved his fertility?"

Ah, Wulfstan thought to himself, keen to hear what others said, and yet there was no time, for the final ealdorman, a man that Wulfstan knew a great deal about, strode to the dais.

He exuded fury, and Wulfstan was, once more, surprised. This was not his understanding of how events would happen that day, and yet Ealdorman Ælfhere thought himself triumphant. That much was clear to see in his gloating stance, as he watched Ealdorman Æthelwine with a modicum of surprise.

He was the son of Athelstan, known as the Half-King for the great trust and respect that he'd earned from the kings he'd served. He'd been the greatest friend of King Edmund until his untimely death in 946, and he'd been foster-father of the future King Edgar, Edmund's youngest son and the soon to be new king's father.

The family ties were close between the House of Wessex and those of Æthelwine, and yet some power play had taken place, and Æthelwine had been left out of it all. He'd been the staunchest supporter of King Edward, Æthelred's half-brother and had stood by his side no matter his irrational actions. He'd been vocal in his support for the youth. Very vocal.

Only then Ealdorman Æthelwine opened his mouth, his words clear for everyone to hear, so that no one needed to strain, or hold an ear to the front of the hall.

"This man stands before you and speaks of matters he little understands. He does not have ancient, royal blood. His family name is little heard of a generation back, and yet he speaks as though he understands what it is to hold such a heritage."

There was no one within the hall whose mouth didn't drop open in surprise. Ealdorman Æthelwine, so the general gossip ran, hated his sister-by-marriage, and had worked tirelessly to undermine her role as Queen while her husband had lived. Indeed, it had been Æthelwine who'd ensured ætheling Edward became king after his father's death, and not Æthelred.

"Damn," Ælfwine whispered, and Wulfstan glanced once more at him. His face was a myriad of reds. Perhaps, after all, Ælfwine was going to be forced to understand the tendencies of the political elite to say whatever they thought would get them the support they needed. Whatever Ælfwine had been promised in exchange for his support, Wulfstan suddenly knew that he was unlikely to get it.

Still, Ealdorman Æthelwine spoke.

"It is the responsibility of those born with such close connections to the ruling House of Wessex to protect that dynasty, not to usurp it."

"Even if those men would be better able to rule?" Ealdorman Ælfhere countered angrily.

Ealdorman Æthelwine seemed to grow in stature as he opened his mouth to speak. He was dressed in beautiful clothing, from his tunic right down to his boots, or so Wulfstan mused. His clothing was clearly cleverly embellished with jewels for he almost glowed where he stood. None could have failed to notice him, even if he'd not been the standing on the dais.

"We men and women of the Witan are given a special and unique place in the rule of our kingdom. It's not our right to usurp the rule or claim powers of governance that we have no right to. The House of Wessex rules England and rules it well. And England is so strong, and powerful, thanks to the House of Wessex, that for a mere handspan of years, it can protect its young heir. I speak for ætheling Æthelred, I name him as my choice of king, as is his right."

By now, everyone within the hall understood what had just happened, and Wulfstan found himself unable to draw his eyes away from the strange tableau playing out before him. Even gasping when the final part of Ealdorman Æthelwine's performance took place. The older statesman, in all his finery and with all the decorum and statesmanship of a man who knew his value, strode the few steps to the young child, and took to his knee his head bowed.

Neither was he alone, soon even old Archbishop Dunstan had followed suit, and Wulfstan watched as from the side of the dais an elegant arm reached out and encouraged Æthelred to take the acclaim of the Witan, as he was formally declared the King of England.

It seemed to Wulfstan as though a wave flooded through the hall then, as row upon row of men and women followed the actions of the premier earl of England, the greatest churchman, and even the new King's mother, as they all stumbled to their knees, heads so low they almost touched the floor.

"Damn," Ælfwine muttered once more, as he too followed the action, proclaiming, in his own small way, the child, Æthelred as the new King of England.

Wulfstan also took to his knee, in imitation of his lord. His head throbbed with all the tiny details he'd been trying to absorb since Ælfwine's first meeting with Ealdorman Ælfhere only a week ago. Ælfhere had made it clear that Ælfwine wouldn't survive long at the Witan unless he knew all the tangled histories of the men and women who held sway there. But hearing the names and seeing the people in the flesh put a whole new slant on what they knew, and even in just the space of a week, much seemed to have changed, and not to Ælfhere's advantage.

As Wulfstan's head swivelled from side to side, when everyone was once more on their feet, trying to place all the names with faces, he wished Ælfwine were doing the same instead of focusing on the interplay between Ealdorman Ælfhere and Ealdorman Æthelwine. That part of the puzzle was the most obvious of the split in the Witan. It was the more subtle undercurrents he needed to understand.

They all needed to understand.

Wulfstan became aware that Ælfwine's attention was focused almost exclusively on the Queen and that she, from time to time, met his gaze.

Wulfstan wondered what it all meant but didn't have long to wait when Lady Elfrida summoned Ælfwine to her presence early the next morning.

"My Lady Elfrida," Ælfwine began, bending low to honour her in her private room.

"Ah Ælfwine, my thanks for coming so promptly," she responded, her voice warm as she glanced first at Ælfwine's face and then to where Æthelred was being instructed by one of her priests. The look gave Wulfstan the clue he was searching for, but it passed Ælfwine by.

"It's my pleasure and an honour," he continued in an overly bright voice. The queen's hair still shone in the candlelight, despite her years, and her face was clear and smooth, no wrinkles yet tracking around her alert eyes.

"As it should be. And your son? He is well?"

"He is growing well my Lady. My thanks for your concern."

"How old is he? I'm afraid the years go too quickly, and I forget."

17

"He is nearly eight, and whatever years have passed, have had no impact on your beauty."

"Excellent," she said, ignoring the comment about her beauty although she smiled to hear it. Ælfwine nodded encouragingly, and Wulfstan tried to swallow the bile in his throat.

"He's a bright boy and is simply in need of a good mother."

A delighted peal of laughter issued from her mouth and Wulfstan winced to hear it.

"Well, I can't help you with that I'm afraid. But, I could perhaps offer him a foster-mother."

Wulfstan held his breath.

"My Lady Queen?" Ælfwine enquired, and suddenly the eyes of everyone in the room focused on him, even the young king because his voice had risen over loudly with shock.

"Your son, Leofwine, I'd like to foster him with Æthelred. He'll need boys his age to grow up with," she said, pausing to gaze fondly at the only child she'd borne for her second husband to survive past early childhood, "and then one day your son will be assured a position of respect and prominence within the Witan."

"My son," Ælfwine stuttered, caught off guard and Wulfstan considered stepping in to help his Lord, especially when he heard the titter of laughter from one of the women, but instead he watched with embarrassment as Ælfwine tried to extract himself from the conversation.

"My Lady Queen, your offer, my son." He stuttered and then stopped and started again.

"My Lady Queen, your offer is most generous, and I only wish that I could accept it." The Queen's face lost its warmth at his words, and Wulfstan wondered how Ælfwine managed to speak in the face of her obvious wrath.

"I mean no offence, my Lady Queen, but my son." He took a deep breath, fiddling with the cuffs of his tunic and trying not to meet her eyes. "My son is all I have. My wife. She died soon after birthing the boy, and I intend to keep him close to me."

The Queen's face softened the smallest bit, and she almost

smiled.

"I won't deny that I'm upset, but the boy is perhaps too young anyway. I would ask that you consider it for the future and Ælfwine," she said, pausing briefly to consider her next words, "I'm touched by your love for the boy. I thought it was only mothers who cherished their children so tenderly."

Ælfwine bowed then, and backed his way out of the room, his eyes flashing between his new young King and the Queen. Wulfstan wondered what he'd been thinking but found out soon enough when they were back in their lodgings.

Ælfwine turned on him, his anger evident in his stance and his intense stare.

"Why didn't you warn me?" he demanded, while the three other men of their group looked on with interest, disturbed from their game and their drinking. Ælfnoth, Leofgar and Brithelm were as new to Ælfwine's leadership as Wulfstan was.

"I tried my Lord. I've mentioned that you need to be careful around Ælfhere. He and the queen were close and think only of how to keep hold of their power. Ælfhere's already made a claim on you, and now the Queen has tried to make it more absolute. I assume that Ælfhere toyed with you, planted the idea that the queen might wish to marry you so that you'd be amenable to his plans. The Queen's a beautiful woman and could have any man she wants, but I think she hopes to carry on ruling in the name of her son. A husband might hamper her; add to the tensions already running through the Witan. I do wonder," and here Wulfstan paused and gulped around his next words, "why you would think the queen might want to marry you."

"And my son," Ælfwine screeched as though he'd not heard Wulfstan's words. "He's not to leave my side, ever. I've made that clear."

Wulfstan was simply relieved that he didn't seem to have heard his words.

When Ælfwine finally slept that night, in a drunken stupor, Wulfstan sat and glowered at the fire. He considered leaving there and then. He'd not made his vow of loyalty so that he could be abused and shouted at when things went wrong. No, he'd made his pledge out of genuine respect for Ælfwine. It was apparent that the feeling wasn't mutual.

Only he didn't leave, instead standing stoically by Ælfwine on the final day of the Witan, enduring the knowing smirks and slightly haughty looks from the queen and her supporters. Wulfstan, unhappy as he was about Ælfwine's behaviour, was at least reassured to see him holding his own after such a shocking miscalculation.

CHAPTER 2 –
APRIL AD978

Kingston Upon Thames

Wulfstan watched the interplay between the chief
men of England with a jaundiced expression on his
face. He was getting sick and tired of the backstabbing and complaining going on between them all. Just a month
since the death of Edward, or the murder of Edward, depending
on who he spoke to, and the ealdormen and churchmen were
unsure of each other, begrudging of allowing any to gain any
ground and mindful of making alliances for they could make
one with the 'wrong' person.

King Æthelred, no matter his intentions at his first Witan, had
been cast almost into oblivion in a very short space of time, Ealdorman Æthelwine and his mother ruling in his name. Wulfstan
fully pitied the boy. Whereas before the sight of such an accomplished Æthelred had made him despair at his son's more child-
like mannerisms, he was now pleased his sons were on the farm
with their mother. They'd have a childhood after all. Æthelred
never would, and Wulfstan knew it wouldn't take long until he
was resentful of his mother's influence and that of her favourite
ealdorman.

Less than a month and he wondered and worried about the

sort of King Æthelred would one day be, just as he'd worried about his older brother before his death. Would he ever be able to make his own decisions? He was ten now, still classed as a child, and he was still an unknown.

It was clear that he'd be crowned king. The Coronation was about to go ahead with as much pomp and ceremony as possible. Ælfwine, riding high in Ealdorman Ælfhere's estimation despite his embarrassment with the Queen, had been kept informed of every little argument and point of contention.

Wulfstan was bored to death with the minutiae and would be pleased when it was all over and done with. He also hoped that Ælfwine would have something else to talk about soon as well. The Coronation was all about one day, nothing more. Æthelred was already acknowledged as the king whether he was crowned or not. The problem was the people who ruled using Æthelred's name. It was that simple.

The new King's father had been consecrated by a handful of bishops and an Archbishop, his elder son by a small number of bishops. But twelve bishops and two archbishops would consecrate the younger son. It wasn't lost on Wulfstan that this was every bishop and archbishop currently holding office within the land. He was surprised they'd not found functions for all the abbots to fulfill as well.

It had taken all of Ealdorman Ælfhere and Æthelwine's skill to bring about the coronation so quickly, and Wulfstan knew that the men fluctuated between being smug about it all, and terror that someone would upset their careful plans and the balancing act they'd been forced into making.

Whatever had happened to the previous king, Ealdorman Ælfhere was as angry as everyone else about it. There were rumours that he planned on removing the dead king's body from his hasty burial site and rehousing it somewhere far more suited to a crowned king. It spoke of a guilt conscience to Wulfstan, but he held his tongue, not wishing to incite another rebuke from Ælfwine.

Wulfstan wondered if Æthelred resented the older man's constant interference or whether he saw him as someone who might protect him? While no one had come forward and been punished for Edward's death, unease persisted amongst the great men and women who ruled the land. After all, if the king could be murdered, then so could everyone else!

The church at Kingston upon Thames was filling quickly, and Ælfwine gestured urgently for Wulfstan to join him. He'd been waiting and watching, as Ealdorman Ælfhere had demanded, but now they were almost too late to make it inside before the ceremony began.

He could hear the voices of the monks raised in song, and he took one last look at the beautiful early summer day before going inside the cavernous building. He doubted he'd see much more of it. The ceremony would be long and tedious as every churchman needed to have his say. Wulfstan wished Ælfwine hadn't demanded his attendance. He'd much rather be outside enjoying the festive mood infecting the small town where an impromptu market had sprung up. Anyone not attending the coronation was bound to end up penniless or drunk by the end of the day.

"Hurry up," Ælfwine hissed at him as he joined him and Wulfstan suppressed an annoyed response. Their relationship was strained. Ælfwine's total acceptance that he was now Ealdorman Ælfhere's adherent was against everything Wulfstan had expected from him when he'd become his commended man. He chafed at the constraints and the new duties being thrust upon him.

He'd thought he'd be little more than Ælfwine's trusted warrior. He'd not realised he'd become his confidant and constant sounding board.

"I'm coming, my Lord," Wulfstan replied, his anger showing in his own hissed words and Ælfwine couldn't fail to hear it although he didn't respond. Then they were inside the church, and everyone was waiting expectantly for the king.

They didn't have long to wait before the holy men made their way into the overly full church, their rich ceremonial clothing draping from their bodies, and between them, the young king, Æthelred.

Æthelred was a slight child, and it was thrown into sharp contrast as he followed the far senior bishops and archbishops, their hair greying while Æthelred's shone as though he was lit from within. Wulfstan thought he'd benefit from some time spent with his household troops. That way he'd develop the muscles he needed to be a physically strong king. He'd also prefer to see him devoid of his richly decorated clothing. If that was what a king had to wear then, Wulfstan was pleased he was no king.

The tunic was heavily embellished with glittering jewels and threads, looking so stiff that Wulfstan wondered if the lad could move his arms from side to side or whether they could only go forwards. His eyes held pride and amusement as he swept between the assembled crowd and Wulfstan found himself infected with the boy's obvious joy at his coronation, despite his anger at Ælfwine. Perhaps, after all, listening to Ælfwine for the best part of the past month had been worth it.

Surprisingly the ceremony passed quickly and to loud cheers, Æthelred was proclaimed as king. His grin of delight was difficult to ignore and yet Wulfstan felt his good mood evaporate when he glanced at the expressions of the ealdormen. Ealdorman Ælfhere was trying not to look too pleased with himself whereas Ealdorman Æthelwine looked pensive. The Queen simply looked as delighted as her son.

During the feast that night, held in honour of the coronation, Ælfwine sat beside Wulfstan, an amused grin on his face.

"Ealdormen Æthelwine and Ælfhere did a good job?" he questioned, but it was more of a statement, and Wulfstan found himself nodding without thinking. He'd been doing a lot of that recently.

"Well, the king's been crowned, so they must have done," he finally relented.

"Ah, don't give me that shit Wulfstan. Tell me what you think."

"Why is that allowed now?" he asked abruptly, pleased to see Ælfwine flinch at the words.

"Wulfstan, don't be like that. I'm sorry. It's been a difficult month."

Wulfstan turned away from Ælfwine, his face thoughtful as he watched the King, the Queen and the six Ealdormen being feasted.

"Not only for you, my Lord," Wulfstan muttered, but Ælfwine heard him all the same.

"Everything should be more settled now. The Ealdormen have reached an accord. The King is crowned. There's no heir yet, and that might cause a problem, but provided the king's kept safe what can go wrong now?"

Wulfstan ideally wanted to argue with Ælfwine but when he put it so succinctly it was difficult to.

"He'll need a wife."

"Well that goes without saying but why should that cause a problem?"

"Ealdorman Ælfhere will want his daughter to marry the king."

"Ælfhere's daughters are all married and far too old unless a husband dies, there's nothing he can do."

"It won't stop him," Wulfstan cautioned, but Ælfwine simply laughed.

"Nothing's going to stop him. Not until Æthelred can rule on his own. I know that everyone knows that. I just need to ride it out until then."

"Is that what you're doing? Riding it out?"

"Of course it is. Why, what did you think I was doing?"

"Oh, I don't know. I thought you were moving in with Ealdorman Ælfhere."

"Well, I'm not. I was just showing how grateful I was." Ælfwine's voice was calm as he spoke, despite the fact that Wulfstan knew he was purposefully trying to rile him.

"Good. It'd be nice to have you back to your usual self."

"What's that supposed to mean?" Ælfwine snapped, but the

King was on his feet, and as the roar of so many people in one small space subsided to nothing, Wulfstan managed to bite back his own angry response before everyone heard it.

"People of England," Æthelred began, his voice loud and high and a few voices cheered the king. Ælfwine grinned beside Wulfstan as if this speech was something he'd orchestrated himself.

"I'm proud to be your King, and I thank you for your support, and I pledge myself, as your King, to ensuring that justice will always be done and that the rights of every man, woman and child in our great land are always upheld. And I can only do so with the support of my ealdormen," and here he nodded towards the men who flanked him, "and the bishops, archbishops and abbots," and here he swept those men a glance. The lad's calm demeanour impressed Wulfstan. Only half a day ago he'd sat before those assembled here and pledged himself as their King and been made more divine than any man or woman, and now he was both reminding them of that, and making himself one of those people once more.

Wulfstan allowed himself to be enthralled.

Perhaps the lad had more about him than the heavy presence of his mother and the warring ealdormen might imply.

"He'll be a good king," Ælfwine said when the cheers died down, and Æthelred sat back down.

"Well see," Wulfstan said. He was still too much of an unknown for Wulfstan to think either way. The little sparks of the lad that he saw, he believed in, but they were too little and too often his mother or one of the two major ealdormen stepped on his toes.

CHAPTER 3 – AD981

Deerhurst

Wulfstan watched the young Leofwine with amusement. The lad was trying hard to follow his father's exacting instructions with the half sized sword and shield, but still, he was all arms and legs in the gentle afternoon sun, and Wulfstan could see the boy's face getting angrier by the moment.

He wanted to be as good as his father, but he didn't yet have the skills, the stamina or the mental capacity to out-think anyone and certainly not his father. Ælfwine might well be a poor man to have in a room of devious men and women plotting intrigue but he more than made up for it when faced with an enemy he could see, hear and slay.

The short training sessions that Ælfwine and Leofwine shared, while frustrating for the lad, were doing wonders for Wulfstan's own technique. Older and wiser than Leofwine, he understood exactly what Ælfwine was trying to teach; the intuitive leap between knowing what to do and being able to put it into action before your opponent could change their intended move.

Wulfstan was not alone as he watched. The rest of Ælfwine's small household force was also there to watch and learn, and sometimes to bet on the likely outcome. It was a source of much pride to Leofwine that on more than one occasion he'd beaten his father and made some money for the two loyal men who always wagered on him, Ælfnoth and Brithelm. This time, though Ælfwine was being less tender with his son and was testing his growing skills.

The summer weather was mild and pleasant, and anyone who could have found some task to see to outside the great hall, that now smelt a little less of freshly cut wood and fresh turf for the roof and a little more like a house that had some permanence.

Ælfwine had spent much of his time and energy on providing the best he could for his son and his followers, and Wulfstan wasn't the only one to appreciate the care lavished on the house. Neither was the hall the only building that Ælfwine had caused to be built. A new sunken grain store, and new sheds for the animals during the winter months had also sprung up, and the farmers who worked the land were also having new homes built.

It was a pleasant and prosperous smallholding, and Wulfstan thought it was just about perfect. At the end of the summer months, Ælfwine planned to have a steep ditch built around the central part of his residence. It was a holdover from the days of the Viking raiders, and one that Wulfstan wasn't sure needed doing, but all the same, he knew he'd bend his back to the work willingly.

The earlier difficulties in his friendship with Ælfwine had resolved themselves. Staying away from the Witan had helped. Ælfwine still made himself available to Ealdorman Ælfhere whenever he was summoned, but secure in his place as one of two premier ealdorman. Ælfhere had become less demanding on him, and Ælfwine had happily stopped offering to do anything that was extra to his usual duties.

Ælfwine seemed happier as well and more secure in himself. In a drunken stupor one night, he'd laughed until he'd cried recounting his misguided attempt to court the Queen. He'd admitted, finally, that Ealdorman Ælfhere had talked him into making the offer of marriage to the King's mother and that his head had been turned by her beauty and her beguiling ways.

After that, the incident had never been spoken of again, and Wulfstan was pleased. Ælfwine was a good man, a good lord. He was Ealdorman Ælfhere's commended man, just as Wulfstan was Ælfwine's, but he was better in his role as Lord. He listened attentively to all those who came to him with complaints or praise, and he did what he could to assist everyone.

The terrible portents that had been much whispered about during Æthelred's first year as King had faded away to mean nothing. The lad was doing as well as he could. The Witan, while not always calm, was at least orderly. Wulfstan hoped two things; that he never had to go to another Witan and that Æthelred would prove to be a good King, able to overstep Ealdorman Æthelwine and Ealdorman Ælfhere when the time came.

He doubted he was the only man to notice how Ælfhere had aged of late. Well into his fifth decade, he no longer moved quite so sprightly, and when Ælfwine did respond to his summons and attended upon him, it was more often than not to hear an old man reminiscing about his youth and the skirmishes he'd been in as a boy. When not discussing the past, he was to be heard discussing the future and the prayers that would be said on his death, by whom and where. He had a great fondness for the monasteries at both Glastonbury and Abingdon and had bequeathed land to them. His brother had retired to become a monk at Glastonbury and Wulfstan thought Ælfhere might be jealous of him.

Wulfstan thought it ironic that the one thing Ealdorman Ælfhere had spent so much time trying to do, bringing about his choice for the kingship, once completed, if not entirely to his tastes, had robbed him of his desire to do more. He'd done what he wanted, and now it was almost as though he waited to die.

Now it was Ælfric, Ælfhere's brother-in-law who did most of the heavy-duty work, standing in for Ælfhere when he was too ill, old, or simply tired, to carry out his duties.

With an eye to the future, Wulfstan hoped that Æthelred was preparing to take firm hold of his kingdom. Once Ælfhere died, the other ealdormen would unite around their King for there'd be no one to cause difficulties. The party of Ealdorman Æthelwine would have power, no matter what the Queen tried to do.

The land lay quiet under the young King, and Wulfstan felt as though England itself was on the cusp of an extended period of peace. The land of the Scots was peaceful on the border and, although it had taken a long time, the Viking Kings of Dublin seemed to have realised that York was no longer a part of their patrimony. Since the expulsion of Eric over twenty years ago England had been whole and united.

The next closest neighbours, the men and women of the ancient Britons, or the Welsh as some referred to them, were on mostly friendly terms with the English King and his ealdormen who ruled the lands adjacent to them.

There had been some odd skirmishes the year before, a small rising in Chester and an attack on Southampton by a disgruntled ship full of men from Norway. Many had been slain in Southampton resulting in the defences of the place being reinforced, much as Ælfwine planned to do on his small landholding.

Still, as he watched the young Leofwine train with his father, he thought that Ælfwine was correct to teach his son to fight. Peace could make a man lazy and complacent. With nothing to keep a man on the edge, ever ready for action, it was likely that he'd forget those important tasks that kept him and his family safe.

A crash of metal on wood and Wulfstan was applauding Leofwine, who turned with a triumphant grin on his young face, a streak of sweaty mud running down his nose. Ælfwine was looking at his son with interest, surprised by the manoeuvre that had sent his sword out of his hand and flying through the air, and allowed his son to work his own sword behind his father's shield.

"Has Wulfstan been teaching you again?" Ælfwine puffed through his cheeks. He was just as hot and sweaty as his son who was dancing from side to side, his pride bursting from him.

"No father," he answered, his voice high and bright, his eyes shining.

"You pulled that move on Wulfstan a few weeks ago in training, and I've wanted to try it ever since."

Ælfwine's eyebrows shot up with shock as he tried to recall the event and then he grinned at his son and offered him a thump on his thin shoulders.

"I didn't realise you watched so carefully?"

"I always watch you, father," Leofwine trilled and then turning to gaze longingly at the river that flowed close to the house, he threw his training equipment to the floor. "I'm going to cool off in that," he shouted, and before anyone could gainsay him, he was gone, streaking across the dusty practice yard.

The gambling men were arguing noisily amongst themselves as they exchanged their coins once more.

"He'll be a good warrior," Wulfstan called to Ælfwine, where he was setting his son's sword and shield to rights.

"I wish he didn't have to be, but, I think the peace we have now is nothing more than a thing of illusion."

They'd talked about this before. They both shared slightly differing views of the future.

"I know Ælfwine, but, well, I wonder who'll come for the English next. The Vikings were nothing more than a transitory thing. They came, they tried to fight us, and those with any sense just settled down, had children and learned to live with the rules the English had, or made it their place and had their own rules made into laws."

"So it was a conquest by fucking?" Ælfwine laughed.

"No, it was an integration through good sex," Wulfstan laughed. This was an old argument and one that neither of them ever won. It had begun one night, when both far too drunk for their own good, had tried to fathom out the reasoning behind the Viking attacks that had thrown the old kingdoms into disarray and from which the resulting 'England' had emerged from the ashes.

"England is rich and prosperous. I can see the appeal," Wulfstan offered as an afterthought and Ælfwine was nodding absent-mindedly as he listened to the joyful splashing of his son in the shallow summer river.

"Your sons?" Ælfwine asked quietly, but Wulfstan turned away from his friend's open face.

"I know you mean well, Ælfwine, I do. But really, it's not something I wish to speak about. Not today."

"But you must miss them?" he pressed, and Wulfstan felt the familiar empty ache in his heart all over again. It never went away. Why would it? Sometimes it was less painful. Through the dark of winter, he brooded on his fate, blaming himself for the choices he'd made and for the decisions he'd allowed his once wife to foist on him. Then through the summer months, he tried to forget about it all, forget he'd ever been a parent with his old family to fend for.

"Of course I miss them," he growled, his voice angrier than he'd intended.

"They could come here…"

"I know all that, but I gave my word, and I intend to abide by it. She makes no other demands on me."

"I hear rumours, though," Ælfwine continued but Wulfstan walked away, towards the sound of Leofwine and his friends in the river.

His two boys might be out of his reach, but they were never far from his mind, no matter how he tried to fool Ælfwine, and he did all he could to fill the void in his life. Leofwine and he were not friends, not yet, but maybe one day the lad would see him as more than the forbidding Wulfstan, the warrior he watched like a hawk but who he rarely spoke to, unless, as just before, he knew he'd done something worthy of praise.

The rumours about his once wife worried him, but his sons were old enough to fend for themselves if they needed to, and more than anything, he didn't want to have to face the woman's wrath. His wife had made it clear that she intended never to see him again, and whatever it was that had warped her mind towards him, he didn't need to experience it again. They were separated, strangers, but his sons knew where he was and they could come for him if they ever needed him.

He doubted they would.

They'd both sided with his mother, not him, and he'd not had the heart to argue with them anymore. It was one thing to see the disgust on her face, quite another to see it on his sons as well.

"Apologies my friend," Ælfwine said when he came to stand behind him some time later. The sun had moved swiftly through the summer sky, but Leofwine and Oscetel still played in the rapidly flowing shallow river, unaware of the passage of time and Wulfstan had become engrossed in their play. He almost wished he could do the same. It was a damn hot day.

"There's no need, and I appreciate your concern, but I have to do this my way."

"I know, and again, my apologies. I must attend upon Ealdorman Ælfhere and the King within the week. You'll stay here?" Ælfwine asked.

Wulfstan contemplated another trip to the Witan and then he shrugged his shoulders.

"No, I'll accompany you this time. You should take Leofwine with you. Let him see how great men behave."

Ælfwine stilled at the thought of that, his expression pensive. He was over protective of the boy and always would be, but if he were going to push Wulfstan to think of things he'd rather not, then he was happy to return the favour.

"You might have a good point. I'll think on it," he said, offering nothing further.

"Where is it this time?"

"Winchester."

"Again?"

"Yes, the boy seems unwilling to come further north. It makes me wonder about Ælfhere."

"Wonder what about him?" Wulfstan pressed. It wasn't like Ælfwine to speak against him.

"Just how secure his position is. And the Queen's."

"You think he won't come to the lands where Ealdorman Ælf-here holds the most sway?"

"I think exactly that. The lad is not foolish. Not by a long shot. He's just young."

"And what of the Queen?"

"I don't think she has quite as much control over what Æthel-red does as she wants."

Wulfstan was pensive.

"Why what's happened that I've missed?" He'd not attended the Witan last year. He'd been suffering from an injury and Ælf-wine had ordered him to stay at home to recover. Wulfstan had been delighted, but now he wondered. He also wondered why it had taken Ælfwine so long to speak to him about what had happened.

"Oh, I don't know. Nothing and everything. The boy speaks well. He holds his own when the other men debate matters of law and state, and he doesn't do it with any reference to his mother or Ealdorman Ælfhere."

"Well, I think I should come then. I want to see this for my-self. It sounds a little unbelievable. How old is he now? Twelve, thirteen? I can't imagine he knows his mind yet, let alone what's right for England."

In the end, Ælfwine chose to take Leofwine with him. He didn't say anything to Wulfstan about it beforehand, but on the morning of their departure, Leofwine was ready and attentive on his horse, and Wulfstan suppressed a smirk of amusement. He just hoped it didn't mean that Ælfwine would start pressing him about his sons.

Leofwine was a refreshing young voice as they rode sedately through the bright day and Wulfstan found himself riding close enough to the boy that he could join in the conversation. Ælf-wine rode at the front, deep in his thoughts, but the majority of the men were alert to any disturbance after the small Vi-king raid the year before. Ælfwine was taking no chances even though they rode through the centre of England, as far from the coast as it was possible to be.

"Wulfstan," Leofwine called, and Wulfstan turned to meet the eager eyes of the lad, surprised he'd chosen to speak to him.

"Yes Leofwine, what is it?"

"I was asking all the men how many battles they've been in. How many have you been in?"

The boy was young enough to see glory in battle and not the blood and guts, the pain and the loss.

"A few Leofwine. Enough to know what I'm good at, and enough to know that I don't enjoy seeing men die."

"But how many?" Leofwine pressed, and Wulfstan laughed at the pleading tone in his voice.

"Too many my boy and you don't need to hear about it."

"If you don't tell me, I'll never know, and I'll never be a great warrior and leader."

"There's more to being a great leader than being able to swing a shield and a war-axe."

"Yes, but I still need to be able to do it."

"I can't deny that. And if you must know, when I was younger and before I knew your father, I had a number of skirmishes and I made a number of kills."

Leofwine's face curled into an intrigued 'o' at the admission. None of Ælfwine's other men had faced an enemy, and they'd all had to disappoint Leofwine.

"And that's all I'm going to say on the matter. But don't worry. When I train with you and teach you, be assured that I know the tactics and the skills you learn are worthwhile acquiring."

Leofwine lapsed into silence then, but his young face was serious and Wulfstan was aware of the lad's eyes on him throughout the rest of the journey. He held his tongue until they reached Winchester.

"Wulfstan, have you killed more men than my father?" the question was asked quietly enough, but Wulfstan looked at the men who surrounded them with some concern. Much of Wulfstan's past was unknown to these men. Only Ælfwine knew of his wife and his children. Only Ælfwine knew of his time fighting.

"Your father is a nobleman. He's been trained, and he's faced his enemies."

Leofwine rolled his eyes at Wulfstan then.

"You might as well have just said yes."

Wulfstan opened his mouth to argue, but Leofwine skipped away, giving the impression that their conversation had meant nothing, but Wulfstan knew better. Leofwine was looking for role models, and he found his father wanting in some areas. Wulfstan almost pitied the lad. He saw through his father's faults too quickly, although he was prepared to credit Ælfwine with far greater skill with his sword than his son was. He might not have ridden into battle, but he was well trained enough and skilled enough that when the time came, he would carry out his duties well.

The following day the Witan convened in the name of the King and Wulfstan found himself playing nursemaid to Leofwine. The boy was curious and wanted to know everything about the small town and the monasteries and church that it contained. While Ælfwine listened to the debates of the men and women of the Witan, the balanced factions of Ealdorman Æthelwine and Ealdorman Ælfhere, with their two supporting ealdormen each cancelling each other out, Wulfstan was tasked with answering the questions of an inquisitive boy. He thought he had the most enjoyable day ahead of him but he found the constant questions to be draining and in the end he almost wished he'd been forced to go to the Witan.

The two religious minsters, side by side, and known only as the 'new' and the 'old' intrigued the boy and Wulfstan, turning his back for only a moment or two wasn't surprised when he momentarily lost Leofwine and found him speaking to one of the monks.

The man, who must have appeared ancient to Leofwine, although only old to Wulfstan, was delighted by the boy's questions, and the afternoon was spent being taken around the Old

Minster. In that time Wulfstan learned more than he thought anyone needed to know about Saint Swithun and was relieved when Leofwine finally said his goodbyes and announced that they could return to their lodging.

Leofwine spoke almost the entire way back to the King's palace and Wulfstan quickly stopped listening. His head was pounding, and he just needed some time alone with his thoughts. So engrossed were the pair of them that they didn't realise they were back inside the palace grounds until Leofwine walked straight into someone and sent them sprawling to the ground.

With dismay, Leofwine reached out to help whomever it was to their feet, and Wulfstan was alarmed to recognise the young King struggling back to his feet as Leofwine offered his assistance.

While Leofwine offered apology after apology, Wulfstan bowed low to the King.

"My Lord Æthelred," he began, Leofwine belatedly heard the words and on realising who he'd collided with his face drained of all colour.

Neither did Æthelred look as though he was about to be magnanimous.

"My Lord Æthelred," Leofwine began again when the King was back on his feet. "My sincere apologies, I was so caught up in my thoughts that I wasn't looking where I was going."

The young King, his face partially hidden in shadow, still managed to make his eyes flash dangerously in his outraged face.

"Who are you?" he demanded angrily, brushing the imaginary dust from his fine clothes.

"L ... Leofwine my Lord. The son of Ælfwine from Deerhurst."

"Ah," the King said, "I've heard a lot about you, but I never thought for a moment that you'd forcefully mow me down."

"My Lord King," Leofwine was stuttering again. "I ... I'm so sorry, I was talking to Wulfstan about the Saint, Saint Swithun and I wasn't looking where I was going." His tone was engaging and yet Wulfstan knew it wouldn't work and was also at a loss how to make the situation better.

"That much is obvious, and now if you'll excuse me, I need to be about more important business than gossiping in the palace grounds."

"Of course my Lord," Leofwine replied, somehow managing to recover his wits enough that he bowed and sounded deferential at the same time.

"Your father. Tell him I need to see him about this," Æthelred said as he turned to leave.

"My Lord?" Leofwine asked but the king was gone, and the lad was left stunned by what had happened.

"Wulfstan, have I caused trouble for my father?"

Wulfstan was watching the retreating back of the young king with some unease. He wasn't sure exactly what had just happened, but he didn't like it. Not one bit.

"No lad, of course not. The King, he's not much older than you, and his mother helps him rule, with Ealdorman Ælfhere. I'm sure he just wants to speak with your father about another matter."

Turning, the pair made their way back to their lodgings, and although Leofwine soon regained his tongue and continued his chatter from during the day, Wulfstan was barely listening to him. Could it be possible that the King was going to make an issue out of such a small thing?

He was right to worry. The young King got to Ælfwine before Wulfstan had the chance, and Ælfwine's face was like thunder when he walked into their lodgings later that evening. Not that he was angry with Leofwine or Wulfstan, but rather with the king.

Leofwine had finally fallen asleep, and silence rang through their small suite of rooms as Ælfwine gestured for Wulfstan to join him outside.

"What happened?" he asked with resignation written all over his face. He looked drained by his interview with the King.

"The lad walked into the king and knocked him down. He

apologised."

"That's what I thought. It was unfortunate."

"Why, what does the King want?"

"He wants to use it as an excuse to bring Leofwine into his household."

Wulfstan winced at the words. He couldn't understand why people were so keen to separate Leofwine from his father, first the Queen and now the son.

"What did you say?"

"I apologised and told him it wasn't possible. He's fuming and threatening all sorts of damnation on him and me, but he relented in the end. I have to pay a fine and secure the coastline for the king next summer."

"And that will be an end to it?" Wulfstan asked without believing the words himself.

"I hope so. The king .... Well, he seemed irrationally angry about the whole thing, completely out of proportion."

"Do you think he's just trying to exert some independence?"

"I don't much care what it is. I don't like it."

"Have you mentioned it to Ealdorman Ælfhere?"

"No, but he probably knows anyway."

"Will he say anything?"

"I doubt it. He's growing old and tired. I'd be surprised if he can be bothered to get too involved in such a minor thing."

"What about the Queen?" Ælfwine shot Wulfstan a look that contained far too much ambiguity for Wulfstan to interpret.

"No, the Queen has even less power than Ealdorman Ælfhere over the King."

"How old is he now?"

"Who Ælfhere, or the King?"

"The King."

"Thirteen. So nearly old enough to rule."

"Old enough to realise that everyone around him only does as he says because Ealdorman Ælfhere stands behind him. He might be trying to stake his claim to the throne."

"I don't think there can be any doubt about that."

"Is it the best time to antagonise him then?" Wulfstan asked. Perhaps, he thought, it would have been better just to do what the king demanded.

"It might not be, but he needs to understand that men and women won't respond to petty demands and offensive speech. He is our king, yes, but the ealdormen support him and act in his name in the lands he never visits. It's more of a partnership than he thinks and he needs to know that. All the way down to his reeves and his household troops."

"And Leofwine?"

"He doesn't need to know about this. I think it would be best if you and he left tomorrow. I'll think of an excuse for you."

"I'm sorry Ælfwine," Wulfstan said feeling defeated.

"It's not your fault. It's the king. I'm not criticising him. I wouldn't want to be bowled over by the enthusiastic bundle that's Leofwine, but still, they could have been raised as brothers. A little toleration would have been far better than this response. We'll just try and deal with it as quietly as we can, and hope the king forgets all about it."

CHAPTER 4 – AD982

Southern Coast

Wulfstan rode his horse confidently, his weapons within easy reach although he wasn't sure he'd need them. This punishment that the king had decided on for Ælfwine was turning into a more than pleasant jaunt through the countryside. He'd not spent much time so near to the southern coast before and he, despite his misgivings, couldn't help but enjoy the gentle sun of the summer and the cooling breeze that blew across his slightly too warm face.

Ælfwine was silent at his side, their small force of only nine men bolstered by some of the local men so that they numbered near enough to fifty, although Ælfwine was in command. They were keen to ensure that there was no repeat of events of the previous year when Southampton was attacked by raiders and people slaughtered.

The King and his ealdormen had decided that the best way to prevent any further attacks was to have roving forces along the coast, led by local King's thegns and including men who'd been trained in the way of war. That way they could send a strong message to opportunistic hunters if they should be lucky enough to come across them. Wulfstan doubted they'd be fortunate enough to happen upon any raiders, but he thought the idea was a sound one and was happy to be riding with his Lord.

The winter had been quiet apart from Leofwine's constant questions, and Wulfstan was more than ready for a change to his staid routine. The boy had been left at home under the careful gaze of Ælfwine's seneschal, Leofgar. Ælfwine had managed to prevent the boy from learning anything about the King's real displeasure from the incident the previous year, but Wulfstan worried that they were only shoring up trouble for the years to come.

Æthelred had continued to try and flex some of his power throughout the winter but to little or no avail. Ealdorman Ælfhere was keeping a firm grip on the boy, as was his mother.

Not far from Portland, Ælfwine called the men to order, concern on his face. Wulfstan caught up in his thoughts, looked to his Lord with concern, his head flicking from side to side, trying to decide what had worried him.

"What do you see?" he asked. His eyesight was keen but in the glare of the bright summer's sun he was struggling and his eyes teared continually.

"Smoke," was the ominous reply, and Wulfstan tried to look where Ælfwine did.

"I smell it too," Ælfwine added and Wulfstan gripped his horse's reins tighter with his left hand, and fiddled with his sword. It wouldn't do if he weren't prepared.

"Where's it coming from?" he asked, and followed Ælfwine's finger when he pointed towards the sea.

Suddenly the sky darkened, as a bank of dense clouds obscured the sun and then Wulfstan saw it as well. Smoke billowed from three homes, and if he squinted, he could just make out the shapes of men and women running through a small settlement on the small stretch of land that ran between the mainland and the smaller protuberance known as Portland.

"Are we going to attack?" he asked Ælfwine when he didn't speak for long moments.

"Yes we will," he replied, slowly and with consideration. "But I need to determine the best way to mount the attack. I don't want just to scare them off. I want them dead." His voice contained real menace and that surprised Wulfstan. He wasn't aware that Ælfwine had a bloodthirsty bone in his body. But then he remembered. Unlike him, Ælfwine had not been in a real battle in his time. He'd never even killed a man.

"You take half the men and circle from the east. I'll lay in wait for a bit, and then do the same with the other half of the men from the west. Hopefully, we'll trap them between our two forces and annihilate them."

"How many men are there?" Wulfstan asked without agreeing to the plan. He wanted to be reassured that Ælfwine wasn't trying to prove himself when the odds were firmly stacked against them.

"About fifty or sixty. Just one ship's worth. I can even see the ship anchored in the harbour. Why?" he asked, casting a suspicious look at Wulfstan.

"It's just best to have all the information my Lord," Wulfstan replied, without any rancour.

"Fine, as long as that's all it was. Now, take your men and go. I want to stop this attack before it does any more damage."

Bowing to Ælfwine from his saddle, Wulfstan signalled whom he wanted with him. The men all came keenly. They, like Wulfstan, were warriors and household troops, who had spent most of their life training for the opportunity to defend their homeland. He might never have relied on any of these men in battle, but having watched them train with a cynical eye when they'd first joined as one group, he knew that they were well prepared, even if they lacked any real practical experience.

The lay of the land gave Wulfstan pause for thought. The stretch of territory the raiders had landed upon wasn't without its advantages, a small peninsula that stretched out into the sea. It was all well and good Ælfwine ordering them to attack from the east, but it wasn't necessarily possible.

Taking matters into his hands, Wulfstan made a snap decision and led the men further east. He could see where Ælfwine was positioning his men, as close to the small stretch of land that ran between the small steading and the mainland as he could get, but Wulfstan worried that the attackers would simply leap into their ship and escape. Ælfwine had made it clear that wasn't an option.

What they needed was a ship of their own so that they could land on the beach where the men had abandoned their ship in search of plunder.

Wulfstan kept his eyes alert as he rode, looking down onto the shore, hoping that he might see a ship that he and his men could borrow for their attack. Sadly luck wasn't on his side and none of the men and women who inhabited the area could be found to ask if they knew where a ship was. He imagined they were all hiding in their homes or had run to the closest settlement that was better defended than Portland, maybe even as far as Dorchester or Corfe.

The smell of burning was intensifying, and Wulfstan felt the faint stirrings of panic. Ælfwine had been less than clear about his timings, but he knew that in coming so far east he'd used up precious time. He looked out at the beached Viking vessel and wondered what to do for the best.

"Wulfstan," one of the men rode towards him, his face flushed with triumphant. "Come, follow me quickly, I've found a ship. It'll hold about fifteen of us, but if the rest of us hold onto the ship at the side, we should be able to swim alongside it. The waters here don't look too deep."

Wulfstan indicated that the man, his name was Eadwig, should show him what he'd found. Around a small cove, and sheltered from the view of all, they came upon a small vessel, probably used for fishing or for taking small goods to and from the island before them. A young man, his eyes bulging inside his slight head, was watching them approach with equal parts fear and equal parts excitement.

Eadwig shouted to the youth.

"This is Wulfstan, our commander. He'll ask if we can borrow your ship."

The youth was nodding so vigorously, Wulfstan worried his head would slip from his shoulders.

"A' course you can, my Lord," the boy said dipping his head slowly, but Wulfstan was having none of it.

"I'm no lord, my boy. My Lord is over there, on the other side of the raiders. We hope to make a two-pronged attack, him from one side and me on the other."

The boy just continued to nod, before jumping to some attention.

"You'll never all fit in the ship, and you'll want to move the horses from here. When the tide comes in, and it is now, this part of the shore gets covered. Come, I'll show you where to put them for safekeeping, perhaps someone can stay and look after them, I'm a man of the sea not of animals, and I don't want to spook them."

"My thanks," Wulfstan said, his eyes looking over his shoulders to where the plumes of smoke seemed to be getting thicker.

"Is it far? We need to attack soon."

"Oh no, my Lord. Just around the headland, and then you can go with the ship. But be careful. The currents can be tricky, especially when the tide is coming in."

Wulfstan's face creased in worry. The lad might be a man of the sea, but he certainly wasn't.

"Could you come with us? Direct the ship so that we avoid the worst parts."

Something like fear swept across the youth's face but then he straightened his shoulders.

"I'd be honoured to help out. Anything to save the folk over there. I know most of them and I even like some of them," he added as an aside. Wulfstan grinned at his honest admission.

Running to keep up with the horses, Frithuric showed them where to stow them safely, and Wulfstan left one of his old warriors to watch them. The man, Waltheof, met his eyes solemnly and nodded to show he understood why he was being left behind. If the worst should happen, he'd be able to take as many horses as he wanted and rush to the nearest ealdorman and demand more assistance. In this place, it would be Æthelweard he needed to reach, and if not him, then he'd need to go directly for one of the King's palaces and hope he found him there.

Wulfstan and the rest of the small force ran back to the fishing ship and after very little argument it was decided that as many men as possible would hunker down in the ship, while the other's held to the side and tried to keep out of sight. The youth was happy to pretend he was just out on a routine fishing trip, and the men who would almost be swimming, threw their shields inside the small ship, and everyone waded out into the chill, salty water.

Wulfstan found himself in the ship, close to Frithuric, who spoke continually to himself as he manoeuvred the small craft, reciting the way to go. Wulfstan assumed his father or grandfather had taught him the route and that he always spoke to himself on the trip. Either that or it was his nerves. Wulfstan left him to his words and focused on what he needed to do now.

The bottom of the ship was wet, and Wulfstan grimaced as chill, salty water soaked into his clothes. He was going to stink when this was done.

Within sight of the enemy ship Wulfstan saw Ælfwine, ready to attack but hidden behind a nearby dune. He hoped that Ælfwine saw their approach too, as otherwise, this attack could be a disaster.

The men were moving as quietly as they could, but the sea was noisy around them, and Wulfstan winced every time one of the men cursed or sloshed too noisily in the deepening sea. He was convinced that there was no way they'd make it to the shore without being heard.

Frithuric tapped Wulfstan on the arm.

"I'll take her in there," and he pointed to a place further down the beach from the raider's ship.

Wulfstan nodded. It was a good choice. He signaled to three of his men to secure the ship against any who tried to retreat, and the rest of them slunk onto the beach, some wet and others dry, depending on whether they'd been on the ship or not. Wulfstan was wet, though, and so were some of the men from inside the ship. It apparently needed caulking again. Wulfstan vowed to ensure Frithuric was rewarded with the means to do so.

He could clearly see where the raiders had taken control of a small collection of buildings. The smell of smoke was diminishing but the odour of crisping flesh was clear and Wulfstan wrinkled his nose. Just one ship full of raiders and they brought death and destruction to so many others. He felt his anger starting to rise, and he let it. Fighting with aggression was always to be preferred. It added the edge he needed to his clinical and well drilled skills.

He'd spent much of his youth training to be a warrior. It was only meeting his wife that had turned him away from his chosen profession. He was pleased he'd had it to fall back upon when his wife .... Well, he didn't want to think about that now.

He was counting the men in his head as he crept up the shoreline. He could see men outside the main house, some clearly drunk and asleep, tumbling from the grain store, and still more men just stood around drinking and laughing. They seemed oblivious to their impending doom. Well, most of them did, he did count at least five who were vaguely alert, but they weren't looking towards the sea, but rather towards the strip of land that Ælfwine was advancing along.

He and the rest of the men spread out and advanced as quickly as they could. Wulfstan didn't want them to have any opportunity to make the small house they'd commandeered defensible.

He stepped past the bloody remains of a previous skirmish. While the body was no longer there, enough blood carpeted the tufty sea grass that Wulfstan knew extensive damage had been done.

The animals that belonged to the farmer also appeared to have been slaughtered, as their enclosures were empty and bare. He swallowed his anger and took a firm grip on his sword, his eyes on the man lounging against a wicker fence before him, his clothing rumpled and smeared with something that Wulfstan assumed was probably blood.

Silently he rushed up behind him, stabbing him in the back as he did. The man didn't even see him coming. He gurgled deep in his throat and slumped down, his eyes having never seen his killer. Wulfstan pulled his sword clear and cries of outrage rang from the small farm as the rest of the men began their assault.

Wulfstan didn't try to see what was happening, trusting everyone to do their part. Instead, he set his sights on another man and this time encountered some resistance.

The man stank of sweat, mead and smoke, his eyes glazed and a little crazed. Wulfstan decided the man clearly thought he could fight. For all his unsteady stance, he held his weapon of choice, a huge axe, arrogantly, swinging it from side to side. Wulfstan renewed his grip on his shield and deciding it might just be better to get this over and done with as soon as possible, he lifted his shield and slammed it into the nose of the man. Blood gushed immediately down his face and into his open mouth, and Wulfstan followed the movement by ramming his sword into the man's gut before he could recover. He died with a surprised look on his face. Perhaps not quite as much of a warrior as he'd thought after all.

Wulfstan kicked the axe from his hand, hoping it would land somewhere out of sight so that no one else could try to use it.

Wulfstan took the time to survey what his force was doing, and watched dispassionately as startled men tried to rush from the hall they'd taken and dash to their ship. He stepped directly into the path of one man, his trousers not even fully fastened, and his shield hanging uselessly from his right hand as he tried to keep his dignity intact with the left. Wulfstan spat in the man's face and sliced him with his bloody sword.

Undefended and without his mail cloak on, the man clutched his stomach and fell to the ground where Wulfstan promptly raised his booted foot and stomped on his neck, ensuring the man was unable to breathe.

Others rushed past him from the hall, not even stopping to see if they could assist their fallen fellow warrior. Wulfstan let them go. He knew there were others who'd intercept them before they made it to the ship.

Initially, he'd considered ordering the men to burn the enemy's ship, but he'd changed his mind at the last moment. If any of the inhabitants of this small farm survived, they'd need the ship to sell to make good on their losses. Wulfstan knew a moment of doubt when he wondered if he should have been quite so far sighted, but when another man rushed at him, his face filled with hatred and blood and spittle staining his bearded chin, Wulfstan forgot his worries.

This man was the best well trained of all the men he'd encountered so far. He might well look like a deranged individual, but he held his sword and his shield correctly and had taken the time to fling his cloak of mail around his shoulders. Wulfstan settled himself. There would be more to this fight than just a simple thrust of his sword followed by a quick death.

The man began to circle him, and Wulfstan stepped away from the body he still stood over, careful where he put his feet in the small herb garden at the front of the farm. It wasn't that he didn't want to destroy the crop, but more that he could tell the soil was well watered and he didn't want to slip or lose his footing or his boot.

He considered changing his weapon because his hand was slick with the blood of the men he'd killed, but he decided to stay with what had proved to be successful so far. He was good with his sword and his shield. His war-axe and his smaller dagger he could use to great effect but he was a strong man, able to easily manipulate the long sword, either with stabbing strokes or with swinging ones against a shield.

He grinned back at the man, a slow, languid smile that spread over his face like honey over bread. He was going to enjoy this.

His enemy didn't falter. His feet firmly planted on the floor as he moved in for his first strike.

"Who the hell do you think you are?" the warrior shouted, his voice rough and harsh.

"What's it to you?" Wulfstan asked, trying to decide whether to try and cut the battle short by making a preemptive strike or whether he should let the man talk himself out first.

"My name is Einar, from Norway and these are my men, and

I'll kill you for your attack here."

Wulfstan listened with half an ear, and hoping for the element of surprise, he rushed into Einar and slammed his shield into the other man's, trying to force his shield away from his stomach so that he could stab him when his body was unprotected. Einar was too alert though and he stepped aside, preventing Wulfstan from making any contact. He spun carefully on his feet and turned back to face Einar.

"My name is Wulfstan, Ælfwine of Deerhurst's thegn, and I will kill you for the damage you've done here."

Einar laughed then, an abrasive sound that rang in Wulfstan's ears.

"So you are no one. I will not die at the hands of a nobody."

"Who were you expecting?" Wulfstan asked with a sneer, "Because the bloody King isn't coming."

"He's just a child. I didn't expect the King, but maybe someone descended from one of the greats. Maybe from the House of Wessex, or are they all too busy killing each other to be worried about a shipload of men come to seek their fortune in England?"

Wulfstan let the words pass over him without rising to the bait, but he filed the information away for a later time. It wasn't good if England was seen as ruled by a weak king with no family to reinforce his claim to the throne.

"The King is near enough a man now and ready to destroy any who try and take his land and wound his people."

"Hah," Einar laughed. "You know nothing, lackey. Now come. Let me kill you so that I can return to my ship."

"I don't think you're going anywhere today, Einar. And your ship no longer belongs to you anyway."

Einar tried to glance over Wulfstan's shoulder then, to see the truth of those words, but Wulfstan had heard enough. He stepped in close, his shield before him, and while Einar fussed about his prized ship, Wulfstan dropped his sword to the floor and grabbed his smaller dagger from his weapons belt, all without Einar even noticing.

A cry of warning came from behind Wulfstan, but Einar

was oblivious to it, only realising his danger when the dagger pierced his stomach and Wulfstan sliced it cleanly open, hot blood pouring down his hand.

"My ship," Wulfstan spat into Einar's face, as he crumpled to the floor before him, his mouth open in shock, his breath gurgling wetly. Wulfstan knew his face was twisted with disgust at Einar, but he couldn't help himself. Einar was clearly a trained warrior, and yet he chose to use his skills on those who might never have held a weapon before. That was no victory. It certainly wasn't why he'd trained as a warrior.

"Wulfstan," he heard his name being shouted and turned with his small dagger raised menacingly. He relaxed again when he saw Ælfwine's face. He was a little bloodied and was staring with interest at the men Wulfstan had just killed.

"They're all dead," he muttered, and Wulfstan nodded. He felt disorientated and wondered whether he meant the raiders or the farmers. Sensing his confusion, Ælfwine clarified the point.

"The raiders are all dead, but so are the inhabitants of the farm." Wulfstan swallowed around his grief. They'd been too late. Rage blinded him, and he turned and struck Einar with his dagger again and again on the back until sweat blurred his sight, and he felt a hand on his shoulder.

"Come on friend. It wasn't your doing. We've done what we can. How did you get behind them?"

"A ship. We found a man to bring us here."

"Ah," Ælfwine said the confusion clearing from his face. "And the horses?"

"We left them on the shore over there."

Ælfwine turned away then, gazing down at the ship that had been the cause of all the trouble.

"They're like ants the way they scatter from their nest."

"At least it was only one ship, an opportunistic attack."

"Yes," Ælfwine said, but his gaze was fixed on the vast expanse of sea before him. "Maybe we should check. Do you think your ship's captain would scout the area for us?"

Wulfstan nodded as he considered the request.

"I'm sure he would, but he can't alone. He'll need men with him. And my Lord. I'd rather it wasn't me. The sea agrees with me less than battle does, and I only came a little way."

Ælfwine slapped him on the back then, his dirty face creased into a smirk of amusement.

"Wulfstan, you're the finest warrior I've ever watched in battle and yet you're scared of the sea?"

"Not so much scared my Lord. I just don't bloody like it. It robs me of my food and my drink and leaves me feeling weak."

"Surely not just a little journey?"

"Oh no, not then. But whenever I've been forced onto a ship, I've lost the contents of my stomach."

"Very well then. You can stay here and clean up the mess. Burn all the bodies or bury them, whichever is easier and set the farm to some order. I'm sure someone will claim it soon enough."

"My thanks, My Lord," Wulfstan said, bowing his head but Ælfwine gave him a strained look.

"Wulfstan, it is I who should be thanking you. The battle was over before it had begun. It wouldn't have succeeded without you. You need to take more credit for yourself, realise just how important you are."

"My thanks, Ælfwine," Wulfstan said, a faint smile playing on his lips. He wasn't used to being complimented for his fighting prowess.

"Now get out of those clothes man. They stink of the sea."

As Ælfwine walked away, Wulfstan took stock of himself. Ælfwine was right. His journey in the ship, short as it had been, had allowed seawater to soak into his clothes, and he smelt of death and fish. He wrinkled his nose and walked away from the body at his feet. There must be clean water somewhere, he thought as he walked. Otherwise, the inhabitants wouldn't have survived.

The other men of Ælfwine's command were busy pilfering the bodies of the dead and taking anything of value. Wulfstan let them have their way. He didn't want anything from the men. It was probably all stolen and belonged to someone else anyway. The words of Ælfwine were all the reward he needed. He only hoped that the King would look more favourably on Leofwine now. Ælfwine had done him a great service.

CHAPTER 5 - AD983

Brycheiniog

T he prowess of Ælfwine's small fighting force led to them being feted and welcomed by the king and the ealdormen, and Wulfstan held out hope that the king might forgive Leofwine for his transgression of the year before. Still, for the time being, Ælfwine decided to keep Leofwine away from the Witan. He argued that it was far better to have him out of sight and out of mind than have him paraded in front of a young King who was too unsure of himself.

The renown the force gained was unwelcome for Wulfstan. He didn't relish killing men, well, not if he had a choice. When Ealdorman Ælfhere announced he was leading a raiding force into Dyfed, it was to Ælfwine and Wulfstan that he first turned, as soon as he'd arranged the support of his household troops.

Sending a messenger ahead to the house at Deerhurst, he more ordered, than requested that Ælfwine joins him on his foray for the king.

"But why? What's their king done?" Wulfstan asked once more. Ælfwine didn't have the answer, and his frustration was growing with Wulfstan's obstinacy on the matter.

"I don't know. Ealdorman Ælfhere didn't say. But we have to go. It's not a request."

"But Ælfwine, your home is far closer to the border than

Ælfhere's. It's more likely that there will be retaliatory raids against you than against Ælfhere if it doesn't work, particularly since the enemy is Einion. He's King of Dyfed, not Gwynedd which borders with Ealdorman Ælfhere's sphere of influence."

"It'll work Wulfstan. Don't worry about it."

"It's not even our war?" Wulfstan pressed, but Ælfwine dismissed his arguments.

"I know all that Wulfstan. Still, we'll go as Ælfhere asks. Hywel has been an ally of his for years, and King Einion is encroaching on his land. Hywel would do the same for us if we came under attack."

Wulfstan wasn't quite as convinced as Ælfwine, but then, he was still unsure of Ealdorman Ælfhere. It had only been a handful of years since Æthelred's accession, and while the Witan seemed to be fairly evenly spread, he was still uneasy. Æthelred, as had been shown two years ago, needed to be managed more. He didn't think that Ælfhere or the King's mother was fulfilling that role adequately.

"Where are we mustering?" he asked, knowing it was useless to argue with Ælfwine.

"Brycheiniog."

"Isn't that where they went last year?"

"I don't know exactly where they went last year, but yes, Ealdorman Ælfhere went to Hywel's aid last year as well."

Wulfstan felt unhappy at the thought of the coming battles, but resolved himself to their eventuality and prepared himself as best he could. After the battle of the year before, he was confident of his skills once more, and Ælfwine's as well, but he didn't feel as though they should go looking for a further altercation. Not if they had a choice in the matter.

The ship they'd encountered the previous year had been only one of three that had savaged Portland. The other two had slipped away before they'd arrived but the destruction they'd left had been almost complete. When they'd salvaged the farm they'd done a tremendous service for the community. There had been little enough left to farm and many of the animals had been slaughtered but what little there was had been quickly pressed back into service. The king had made sure that Ælfwine knew how much his service had been valued by sending regular reports from the men and women of the small island and had rewarded Fithuric with new wood to build his ship.

Wulfstan had been to the lands of the Britons once before, before his marriage and the birth of his sons. He remembered it as a land of contrasts, high peaks and deep valleys, blazing heat and fierce winds. He also knew that its ruggedness was a deterrent to the Viking raiders. They preferred their targets to be as easy as possible to reach, as the attack on Portland had proved.

Once more Leofwine was left at home when they rode out with the rest of the men. Leofgar was left behind to defend Deerhurst. They were to meet with Ealdorman Ælfhere near Hereford, a place that was sometimes a part of Mercia and sometimes a part of the kingdom of Gwent. It would allow the men to ride straight into Brycheiniog. But it was also far too close to Deerhurst for Wulfstan's liking.

He didn't relish the thought of going into the disputed territories of the British Kings. They did little but bicker amongst themselves, and as their views were entirely internalised, he wondered why Ealdorman Ælfhere had to become involved with them. Not that this was the first time. Wulfstan knew that for a fact. Ælfhere and Hywel had been allies for some years, even before Hywel had become King of Gwynedd following the capture of his co-ruler, his uncle, who'd then disappeared. No doubt he'd been murdered on the younger man's orders. It was proof, if it was needed, that the dangerous in-fighting that took place within the English Witan was the work of all men everywhere, not just the English.

Still, the English at Mexborough had killed Hywel's grandfather, and Wulfstan questioned how Hywel could now ally with the English. It made good sense for the English to ally with Hywel, but not vice versa. Not that it was a new thing. Hywel had met with the boy king's father only ten years ago and pledged his support to him. Wulfstan wondered if Ealdorman

Ælfhere's alliance stemmed from that meeting. It would make perfect sense if it did.

They came upon Ealdorman Ælfhere and his men at the mustering point near Hereford, and Wulfstan did a double take when he glanced at Ælfhere. He knew the man had been ageing, but now he looked merely breaths away from taking his last one. He was sure he shouldn't be riding to battle. Even Ælfwine shared his concern with Wulfstan and with Ælfhere himself, but the aged ealdorman wouldn't be swayed.

"My ally has called on me to support him, and I will, and you will do as well. Whatever happens to me, happens to me. I should sooner die in battle than in my bed. I'd have become a bloody monk like my brother if I wanted a peaceful death. Now, we won't speak about it again. We have work to do this summer, and if by some chance, we come across some Viking raiders, I expect you to deal with them as efficiently as you did last year in Portland."

So told, Ælfwine readied his band of men for war. The prize was the land of the kingdoms of Brycheiniog and Morgannwg. They were to meet with Hywel inside the lands of Brycheiniog and then devise their plan from there.

King Einion was the intended target. He was a grandson of Hywel Dda; King Athelstan's one-time ally and the man who'd hoped to live a life similar to that of King Alfred. It was clear that the desire to unite the disparate kingdoms of the British ran strongly through the family and Einion had already tried his hand at alienating the land of Gower to himself. He'd been unsuccessful, but still, he'd tried and clearly he was confident in his abilities to try his luck once more, this time in Brycheiniog.

Wulfstan found the confusion of British Kings difficult to keep straight in his mind. Everyone seemed to be related to someone else and they'd all, at one point or another, been allied with the English Kings in recent years. He doubted the loyalty of every single one of them, and that stirred his unease further. This expedition was asking for trouble, and he felt a deep sense of foreboding.

Ælfwine was involved in the war counsels and kept his counsel as well. Wulfstan felt a little ignored but chose not to make an issue of it. Perhaps Ælfwine was just shielding him from the petty arguments two men will have when they're supposed to be allies. He hoped that was all it was.

King Hywel was a man of constant motion. He never seemed to stop, and Wulfstan almost pitied Ælfwine for having to watch him walk backwards and forwards when they were in counsel. When he slept, and it was little, the entire camp relaxed. But it never lasted that long.

King Hywel had sent some of his men to the border with Brycheiniog to meet them, and as they rode through the craggy landscape, through the heat and chill of the magnificent mountains and valleys, faint wisps of smoke tickled his nostrils. Wulfstan knew that the men were already having some success amongst the local inhabitants.

He pitied the men and women of the land. They often came under attack, caught as they were between the kingdoms of the English and the British, both sides hoping to claim more land for themselves. It would have been far better, he often thought, if the lands were simply united under one king, but he doubted it would ever happen. The British and the English were too different to each other, and they were vocal in their differences and keen to pursue those differences. Often too vocally, but Wulfstan wasn't about to mention that to any British he met, or any of the English he served with.

Despite the best intentions of King Athelstan, King Edmund and King Edgar to create a united front against any Viking raiders and to keep everyone safe, the alliances with the kings of the British, or Gwynedd, Powys or Dyfed always disintegrated far too quickly. Admittedly the frequency of attacks on England had diminished to almost nothing, and the strength of the previous kingships could be held responsible for that, but still, there was always someone desperate enough to come and try their luck. Just as the raiders in Portland had, and those in

Southampton the year before that.

King Hywel of Gwynedd was everything that Wulfstan expected a warrior king to be. He was a careful man in words and deeds, despite his constant movement, until he had a sword in his hand, and then it seemed as though he knew every dirty tactic there was to know. When the men trained at the end of a day's riding, he was instantly amongst them all, shouting at them, screaming at them to fight better. And then, just to show how he'd earned his kingship, he'd show them exactly what he meant. He was fast on his feet as well.

Wulfstan watched him with interest, deciding on how he'd attack the king if he were ever given the chance himself. He fought with flair and decisiveness. He never feinted or tried to confuse his opponent. What you saw with him was exactly what you got. And that was part of his skill. Most warriors expected men to try and trick them. When they didn't, it was more of a surprise than if they did.

That night Ælfwine came back to their tent, a scowl of delight on his face.

"King Einion has been sighted just a day away. We'll probably join battle tomorrow or the day after at the latest."

"What here?" Wulfstan asked, perplexed by the choice of battle line. They were in the middle of nowhere. They'd not even passed a home in the last two days. It seemed as though they were fighting for nothing.

"No, but not far from here. But yes, there's no farm or defensive structure to retreat to. Just fields and sheep as far as the eye can see."

"Well, you know me, I'm always happy to fight for a sheep or two," Wulfstan answered darkly, rousing a dull chuckle from Ælfwine.

"Sheep have more value than men, as do cattle; otherwise we'd not spend half our time trying to steal someone else's."

Wulfstan tried not to argue with that logic, but he knew he was feeling sour about this expedition. They'd been riding for nearly a week now, up and down every mountain they came across, and still, there didn't seem to be anything of value to gain from taking this land. There were few people to tithe and few sources of wealth, apart from the sheep and the cattle they came across.

"It's land, Wulfstan. They just want the land so that they can call it their own and add another name to their title. Our kings were like it not so long ago. We've only had York back for twenty-five years, and the people of the Danelaw still hold to their laws and customs, and the king protects those laws."

"I appreciate that but surely, if there were a few more natural boundaries, none of this would be necessary."

Ælfwine arched an eyebrow as he looked at him.

"I don't think your logic quite works Wulfstan. The Vikings have to come across a vast swathe of sea, and yet they still come. They don't let anything stop them."

"Well they bloody should," he muttered to himself. His thoughts were dark and angry. He didn't want to be here. Not again. Last year when he was defending the English people and killing men who wanted to kill them he'd been able to reconcile his actions with his thoughts. Now he really couldn't.

The enemy they faced wasn't even their enemy. He and Ælfwine were just men to hire and that went against everything he'd sworn to do when he'd made his commendatory oath to Ælfwine.

He cast angry looks at the roof of his temporary canvas home and thought of his warm and comfortable bed in Deerhurst. Sometimes he questioned his life choices and didn't like what he discovered about himself. He knew he'd have to kill on this expedition, and the man or men he killed would be someone's husband, father or brother. That didn't sit well with him.

He woke the next morning, his mood as foul as it had been the night before and he sat on his camp bed, holding his sword and thinking of what he might have to do with it later. The stains of the dead men the year before had been easy to remove. He wasn't sure the same would be true about today.

Silently, he readied himself for the day and luckily, Ælfwine kept his peace at his side. Wulfstan hoped it was because he knew how conflicted his thoughts were.

They rode, following the contours of the mountains and valleys as they went, watering their horses at the rivers they came upon, and seeing no people. Sheep were liberally scattered around the summer meadows, and Wulfstan was sure that shepherds watched them, but they made no effort to make themselves visible, and he didn't blame them. A host of over two hundred and fifty men riding through the still landscape was something to be feared not embraced.

King Hywel had sent out a few men to scout where King Einion would be, and around midday two of the men came racing back towards their Lord, their faces flushed and excitement in their eyes.

"Over the next ridge my Lords," they shouted to Ealdorman Ælfhere and King Hywel. "King Einion has stopped and is making a battle line."

"How many men?" Hywel barked as he considered where he and his men were and where the enemy was.

"About three hundred. No more. Unless they're hiding," the first rider said, and Hywel harrumphed at the number.

"He'll have more men, somewhere. But that's nothing for us to worry about right now. We'll ride on as normal and then leave our horses near to the end of the valley. Some of my men will watch them."

Ealdorman Ælfhere agreed without arguing, and Wulfstan felt his stomach swirl uncomfortably. All his doubts and now he'd have no time to consider them. He'd just have to fight as he was being commanded to do.

He slipped from his horse and after a pat on the neck for the animal he reached for his shield and began to form up with Ælfwine and the rest of the men. He breathed deeply for long moments and then they began to move out of the valley in an orderly line, not too fast and not too slow either.

They burst out onto a mountainside bathed in bright summer sunshine, and to the roars of three hundred men ready to attack them. Wulfstan wondered why they'd not tried to block their path through the valley, but he had no time to consider the thought fully. King Hywel was shouting at the men to form up, and already, the enemy was using their swords to hammer on their shields, their impatience clear to see.

Wulfstan eyed the men before him. They were clearly well trained. They stood calmly, but menacingly, and their equipment was shining brightly in the clear day. They'd come to do battle, and they meant to win. Bright helms glittered in the sunshine, and Wulfstan raised his arm to shield his eyes.

Ah, now he understood. They would be facing into the bright sun when they attacked. The enemy had an advantage already, as they'd fight with the sun behind them.

Ælfwine touched Wulfstan's shoulder.

"Good luck my friend. This isn't a battle to die in. Remember that. There will be no songs or poems about this battle. None at all."

Wulfstan grunted as he settled himself beside Ælfwine. They weren't exactly the most inspiring words to hear before meeting men in battle who wanted to kill you.

King Hywel was more encouraging when he roared at his men, demanding they seek vengeance against the traitor King Einion for claiming land that belonged to them. He harangued his men, demanding they make Einion pay for his arrogance in claiming the land, and although Wulfstan felt cold at the words being shouted, the men Hywel had brought with him beat their shields with their swords and raised their voices derisively against the enemy.

Wulfstan shrugged to himself. He supposed a similar appeal to his ideas of what England should be might well have roused him to battle as well. Maybe.

The men hadn't even considered opening a dialogue. It was evident that they'd been set on an attack from the moment King Hywel considered exacting his revenge on King Einion.

"He speaks well," Ælfwine said in an aside to Wulfstan, and

Wulfstan turned to look at him in shock, pleased when Ælfwine met his eyes with amusement on his face.

"I jest you fool. Now remember, don't die here. It's not your time."

With that, King Hywel called the men to advance as did King Einion from his side of the battle line. Or at least Wulfstan assumed that who was leading the men. He could make out no discerning features because he was covered from head to foot in a cloak of mail, a helm and a shield, far bigger than was typically used. He wondered where he'd gotten the idea from that a shield so huge would be advantageous.

Ealdorman Ælfhere wore his battle clothes as well, but he, out of them all, still sat astride his horse at the cleft into the valley where they'd left the horses. He might well be able to ride with the men, but he'd announced he couldn't rely on his old legs to help him fight. He might dream of dying in a battle, but he was unlikely to do so now. He was too old to fight. Instead, he remained at the rear, ready to command if need be, and also, Wulfstan thought acerbically, willing to retreat if King Hywel lost the battle. Ælfhere had also decided that this was not a cause to die for.

King Hywel was far younger than Ealdorman Ælfhere, and he was thoroughly roused to battle, his long hair flaming down his back and his movements precise if predictable. As one they moved forward, one shield against another. Wulfstan knew that while the English men of Ælfhere, all one hundred of them, would hold their places, Ælfwine and Ælfhere had warned all of them before they met with the men of Gwynedd, that they might break the position and choose to fight one on one, and not as a whole unit. Wulfstan had heard of it before but was curious to see it in action.

Not that he had long to wait. No sooner had the sound of the shields clashing against each other reverberated up and down his left arm, than he felt the shield wall give way. He poked his head above his shield in panic. Surely they hadn't broken through the shield already? He was rewarded with the view of the men of Gwynedd and those of Dyfed standing and attacking each other individually, their shields almost discarded at their sides.

He watched with interest for a long moment and then felt a crash on his shield. He looked to its cause and found himself facing a small, wiry man, his dagger in his hand and his axe in the other.

"I'll show you how to fight you English bastard," the man shouted, and Wulfstan felt his eyes open a little in shock. There was a lot of hatred in that sentence, more than this brief skirmish could have caused.

"Likewise, I'll return the favour," Wulfstan hollered, and then he too dropped his shield to the side, and grabbed hold of his sword and his war-axe. It was always better to fight with weapons of equal force.

The man, his black eyes all that was visible behind his helm and nose guard, lashed out with his dagger and Wulfstan stopped the movement with his hammer, entangling the man's dagger in his sword. He was surprised by the strength holding onto the dagger and despite his attempts to trap the weapon, the enemy soon had his dagger free and was slashing at him with the axe.

Wulfstan dodged out of the way, unaware that another fought beside him. He narrowly avoided crashing into the other man by skipping out of his way, and unfortunately into another attack from his enemy. He felt the axe impact his protective cloak, and he cursed this way of fighting. He was used to knowing where everyone was because they stood in as straight a line as possible.

Quickly he recovered and aimed a blow with his sword at the man's left arm. He'd quite like to force him to relinquish one of his weapons. The man saw the move coming and moved out of the way, but Wulfstan followed through and stepped even closer to him, restricting the space between them. With his war-axe, he aimed for the man's exposed neck and almost managed to connect. But the man moved with the speed of lightening and was out of the way and back in position before Wulfstan understood what had happened.

He growled angrily under his breath, focusing his thoughts as he did so. This man was a clever warrior. There was no denying that, and yet Wulfstan knew that he had an advantage over him, if only he could use it.

The bright sunlight flashed in his eyes, temporarily blinding him and forcing sweat to drip down his forehead and into his eyes. He needed to wipe his stinging eyes but couldn't risk relinquishing either weapon he held, even if only for a moment.

The other man noticed his slight stumble and silently moved closer, his short dagger poised to attack Wulfstan's left side. Instead of trying to dodge the attack, which Wulfstan knew he couldn't do in the space of time he had, he fell into the attack, blunting the force of the dagger so that it made no impact on him and in the process surprising the other man. He danced further to the left, hoping to draw the man on, to make him turn around and encircle him so that he faced the bright sun, but the other man wasn't falling for his ploy.

Around him, the sound of battle was deafening. Only just under six hundred men fought on the hillside, but it sounded as though an army of thousands was there, the clash of swords and war-axes echoing eerily through the summer air, coming back as slowly dying echoes, only to be renewed again by the next strokes. The outraged cry of the sheep in the field opposite added a strange new sound to that of the battle.

Wulfstan felt his temper starting to build. It wasn't his fight, and he didn't want to be here, much less have his life in danger. He needed to end it now. With a decisiveness that King Hywel would have been proud of, he sprang forward so that his face was far above the other man's, using his towering form to cut down the options available to his enemy. Before the man even realised what was happening, he'd raised his war-axe and his sword behind the man, as though he was going to embrace him, only to dig the sword into the man's back and use the war-axe to pull at the wound he'd opened up.

He felt the red, hot pulse of the dying man's blood, and he did him the honour of at least meeting his eyes before he tumbled to the ground.

It had been a quick death. The bastard should be pleased with that.

He turned quickly, surveying the battlefield, but he was unable to make sense of what was happening and who was winning without the common indicators of two shield walls.

A handful of men lay dead or dying around him, and he glanced for Ælfwine and found him in close combat with a man who might well have been the brother or cousin of the man he'd just killed. The battle was close and could have gone either way, but he put an end to it by stepping behind the man with his bloodied sword and digging it into his exposed back. The men of Dyfed needed to learn the importance of a shield wall.

Ælfwine met his eyes with anger.

"I was winning."

"You bloody weren't. You were equal, and you know it. Now stop bitching about it and thank me for helping you."

"Bugger," Ælfwine muttered under his breath, and Wulfstan took that as all the thanks he was likely to get.

"What the hell's happening?" he asked of no one in particular. He received no response and took the time to catch his breath and look at the battle site.

Men seemed to be running all over the place, some locked in combat and others just looking on. He could see the men of Dyfed interspersed with the men of Gwynedd, and he wondered how Ealdorman Ælfhere was supposed to make sense of the carnage before him.

The enemy wasn't pulling back but for the time being, no one came to threaten their small group of warriors, and Ælfwine's group of nine men stood amongst a sea of dead bodies and watched with horrified fascination as the battle played out in a way they'd never seen before.

"Even those shipmen of last year were better organised than this," Ælfwine muttered, and Wulfstan nodded in agreement.

Behind them, he heard the whoosh of a horse's breath and turned to meet the appraising gaze of Ealdorman Ælfhere.

"They always fight like this. The idiots. Every time I suggest to King Hywel that he should use the shield wall, he shrugs it aside. Don't worry. It won't last much longer. Look, some of the men are already starting to slink away, and Hywel will be preparing to do the same shortly as well. They don't fight to the death. Just until they've made their point."

Wulfstan looked at the old man with renewed interest.

"So why fight at all, my Lord?" he added hastily, remembering that Ælfhere was not Ælfwine to plague with his questions whenever he wanted to.

"It's the way they fight amongst themselves. Hywel says it's always been like this. These men fight for the honour of fighting, not to gain land. Or at least, I can't see that they do. The only time they gain ground is when the other side can't rouse a force to attack them and then they just walk into each other's land."

"And the people don't mind?" Wulfstan asked, incredulous.

"What people?" Ælfhere chortled, his eyes moving to watch the men who still fought. "There's few enough of them to tax and fewer enough of them to win over. God only knows why the Vikings come here. There's nothing of value, as far as I can tell."

Wulfstan was astounded, but Ealdorman Ælfhere was right. Both sides were starting to bleed away, and while some would never leave the battle site alive, the number of those who'd died seemed to be quite small. Wulfstan kept a firm grip on his shield and his sword.

"Not that this will be the only battle. We'll have a few skirmishes, and then Hywel and Einion will reach an agreement, and everyone can go home."

"So we'll follow them deeper into Brycheiniog?"

"Yes, for a few more weeks."

Wulfstan shook his head at the ludicrousness of this state of affairs. Men died just so Kings and would be Kings could say they'd won a battle. It was a waste of good men and resources, but one that seemed to be accepted by all.

At his side Ælfwine shrugged his shoulders as King Einion and his men ran for their horses and retreated further into the valley.

"They do this every year?" he asked of no one in particular.

"They do. Just like our ancient kings once did. They'll take the animals, and they'll slaughter those they encounter. Then, when the weather changes, they'll go home and harvest their crops and get fat on the stories of their successes."

Wulfstan glanced at Ealdorman Ælfhere one more time, just to check he spoke the truth, but his face was flat, no hint of deceit to be seen.

"Funny buggers," Wulfstan mouthed, and Ælfwine nodded his head in agreement.

"You're not wrong Wulfstan, not at all."

They had fought three more skirmishes before the King of Dyfed and Gwynedd agreed to make terms. Ealdorman Ælfhere was effusive with his thanks to his warriors, and King Hywel was the same. However ineffectual Wulfstan might have thought they'd been, they'd done enough for King Einion to admit defeat and retire from the lands he'd tried to claim.

With delight, King Hywel informed his warriors that King Einion had been overwhelmed by their response to his incursions, and despite his superior numbers, the strength of the combined English and Gwynedd force had surprised him.

Wulfstan was just pleased that the expedition was over so soon. He'd killed ten men in all. A number he found difficult to reconcile with the rewards that King Hywel was claiming, and apparently an unusually large number. Or so King Hywel told him when he had him brought before him.

"I understand your name is Wulfstan," the man said, his gaze fixated on him as though he tried to figure out what lay beneath both his clothing and his skin.

"Yes, My Lord King, and I'm the commander of Ælfwine of Deerhurst's men."

Hywel looked then to Ælfwine who stood at his side, a faint

smiling playing around his lips.

"You're fortunate to have such a skilled warrior amongst your men."

"I am my Lord, and he's not just skilled in warcraft, but statecraft as well. He's an excellent man and I learn much from him."

"I'm sure you do. I'd very much like to have you within my household, but," and here he held up his hand to stop Wulfstan from jumping in to turn down the request, "I understand from Ealdorman Ælfhere that it wouldn't be possible. You have your oaths, and you're a man of honour who'll stand by them."

Wulfstan was surprised to hear that Ælfhere had spoken out for him. He'd never really appreciated that the Ealdorman knew who he was, let alone appreciated that his loyalty and his allegiance was only to Ælfwine.

"Still, I would like to personally thank you and reward you for your endeavours on my behalf."

So speaking, he held his hand out and unfurled it. Within his hand nestled a small golden cross, festooned with ruby jewels at its four points and a larger one at its centre. Ælfwine gasped with surprise beside him and Wulfstan only just managed not to.

King Hywel cast a glance at Ealdorman Ælfhere, an expression that Wulfstan wasn't quite sure of.

"I know the value of rewarding my men."

"My thanks my Lord," Wulfstan stuttered, holding his hand out to take the proffered gift. It felt heavy and cold in his hand, and he glanced from Ælfwine to Ælfhere as though for support. Ealdorman Ælfhere was watching him with an amused expression on his lined old face whereas Ælfwine was nodding encouragingly.

"Men of such skills should be rewarded," King Hywel continued, "even when those men happen to be English."

Wulfstan felt his eyebrows rise at the backhanded compliments but kept his peace. He only hoped that the token didn't make him somehow indebted to the King of Gwynedd.

CHAPTER 6 - AD985

Mercian/Gwynedd Border

Wulfstan reined his horse in and looked back the way he'd come. He was part of a select band of fifty men, once more under the leadership of Ælfwine, but this time doing the bidding of Ealdorman Ælfric. And once more, Wulfstan wasn't at all happy about Ælfwine's role in the upcoming engagement.

King Hywel had proved himself to be a contrary ally and now instead of supporting him, they went to meet him and stop his incursions into the Mercian lands. Diplomacy had failed, and King Æthelred had demanded that if King Hywel couldn't be brought to reason, then he'd have to be stopped using force. Ealdorman Ælfric had chosen Ælfwine as that force.

Someone had been schooling Æthelred in the ways of the past, and he'd been heard to mutter about traitorous grandfathers on more than one occasion, an apparent reference to King Idwal, killed at Mexborough by Athelstan Half-King. Wulfstan doubted there was any going back from the coming war.

He'd much rather be going back than forwards, but once more, he had no choice. Ælfwine had become something of a go-to man in the Mercian lands, and Ealdorman Ælfhere first, and then Ealdorman Ælfric after him, had used them to face down their enemies; Viking raiders, the men of Dyfed and now the men of Gwynedd. It was not what he'd thought he'd be spending his time doing.

His sons were almost entirely grown now but still he missed them and the life he'd thought he'd be living with them. The yearly mustering of Ælfwine's war band was draining him. He'd rather be at the Witan listening to the ridiculous rhetoric of men who thought their opinions mattered than risking his life for causes he didn't believe in.

Leofwine was growing fast, and while his questions had lessened, he watched more now, and he saw everything. Wulfstan sometimes felt uneasy in his presence, as if he knew everything the older man thought and knew when Wulfstan didn't believe the words that were used to mask what was happening, acting as trained warriors and killing any who stood in the way of the peace the King craved.

The boy hadn't been allowed to return to the Witan yet, and Wulfstan had felt Ælfwine was erring in his judgment. Well, he had, until he and Ælfwine had appeared before the King at the Witan the year before and Wulfstan had caught his too keen eye searching for the boy who'd once knocked him down and made a childhood enemy. Then Wulfstan realised that Ælfwine was wiser than him. Sooner or later though Leofwine would need to be fostered and he'd need to come to the Witan. Wulfstan hoped that by then Leofwine would be able to hold his own against the growing force of the King.

Æthelred was grown to manhood as well. He had matured into a better man than Wulfstan had hoped he would, although he still had some doubts. It was better now that he had an acknowledged heir, but the boy was a babe in arms and would need years to grow to maturity. Until then the King was frustrated by his inability to ride out himself, to use the skills that he'd gained when he'd finally been allowed to train with his household troops.

His mother didn't approve, but following Ealdorman Ælfhere's death, she was diminished in her responsibilities and her role. Wulfstan wondered just how much she resented being forced to the back of the political machinations of the Witan. He wondered how she'd work her way back into his affections because there was no doubt that she would. She needed the King more than he needed her and she'd work hard to make it appear vice versa.

Wulfstan could admire her when she wasn't forcing the King's hand, but he did worry about the future.

Ælfwine himself had been shocked and saddened by the death of Ealdorman Ælfhere not long after their attack against King Einion of Dyfed but then he'd breathed deeply and voiced the thoughts that he might be a little freer in his actions. He'd been proved wrong. Ealdorman Ælfric was not an easy master now that he was the Ealdorman of Mercia. He'd expected everyone to continue in their firm allegiance to the role of Ealdorman, even if the man himself had changed. Sadly, he didn't have the charisma of the late Ælfhere and neither did he have the vast connections. He had the ear of the King, but Æthelred was firmly calling himself King now and acting as the King. He wasn't being manipulated by people older and stronger than he was. At least not all the time.

He'd redrawn some of the policies that had been used in his name when he was but a young boy, and in doing so he'd made just as many friends and just as many enemies as he'd always had, but he'd also garnered the respect of the ealdormen. Ealdorman Æthelweard was unusually outspoken in his support for Æthelred, and there was no other reason for it than Æthelweard did believe in the King. He didn't try to gain anything from the King, happy to serve in his capacity of Ealdorman and in his spare moments he worked on his history of the last century. Wulfstan didn't doubt that learning about the past was making him think carefully of the future.

It almost made him wish that he was noble enough to have learnt to read and write, as opposed to how to kill and maim.

"You're quiet today," Ælfwine said to Wulfstan as he sidled his horse next to Wulfstan's.

"Just thinking."

"About what?" Ælfwine pressed.

"The past, and the present," Wulfstan offered a little pretentiously.

"I don't know who taught you to think, but I'd happily inform them that they did me a great disservice."

"My Lord?" Wulfstan asked, perplexed by Ælfwine's words.

"You think too much man," Ælfwine clarified with amusement in his voice.

"And you don't think enough," Wulfstan countered, but Ælfwine was in too good a mood to feel the force behind those words. He chuckled instead.

"Wulfstan you're a serious man, and you know I appreciate that, but sometimes I do wish you'd just smile a little and relax."

"I don't think you should be telling me to relax when we're on our way to carry out murder."

"It's not murder, is it? It'll be a small force, nothing more, and then we'll be released to ride the coast line again."

"And what of Ealdorman Ælfric? Why isn't he here?"

"Well, he'll be off to the Witan."

"Are you not going?"

"God no, I couldn't think of anything worse to do with my time. I'm a man of action. I'm happy in Deerhurst. I've seen what power does to other men, and I don't ever want to run the temptation of becoming other than I am."

Wulfstan nodded his head as he thought.

"I agree with you but wish you'd be more outspoken to Ealdorman Ælfric."

Ælfwine's eyes narrowed a little at that comment, and Wulfstan thought he was about to be rebuked. The words that fell from Ælfwine's mouth more than surprised him.

"Ælfric does himself no favours, and in fact, I sometimes think he acts only to annoy the King. I don't think the ealdorman will be bothering us for long."

Wulfstan had missed all of this as he'd not attended the Witan for the last two years and tried his hardest to stay away from Ealdorman Ælfric when he did call on Ælfwine.

"What has he done?" Wulfstan asked, his voice laced with intrigue.

"Everything and nothing. His biggest problem is that he fails to take account of the fact that Æthelred is now the King and wants to be treated as such. I think he still sees him as a little boy, even though he now has his own in the cradle."

"You've not spoken of this before?" Wulfstan pushed, and Ælfwine sighed.

"I forget you're not always with me and always aware of what I see. I apologise. I just assumed you knew."

"So why are we riding out on his orders?"

"Because they're not his orders. They're the King's, and we do serve him."

Wulfstan subsided into silence then. He'd once chastised Ælfwine for not paying enough attention to events at the Witan. It now seemed that he was guilty of that very mistake as well.

"I should come with you more often," he finally said, and Ælfwine grinned at him.

"You hate the Witan. I hate the Witan. I have to go, but you don't. But, well, if you want to then you can come whenever I'm forced to attend."

They rode on for some time in silence before Wulfstan spoke again.

"You think Ealdorman Ælfric will do something so wrong that he'll end up losing his position?"

"I do yes."

"But who'll replace him?"

This time, Wulfstan didn't miss the glow of interest in his friend's eyes.

"I don't know Wulfstan," he almost sang, "who do you think might be on course to be the next Ealdorman of Mercia?"

Wulfstan's mouth gaped open in shock. After everything Ælfwine had ever said, he honestly didn't expect him to have any designs on the role of an ealdorman.

"You'll have to let your son be fostered out then," he ribbed, and Ælfwine pierced his gaze.

"I know and that, well, that does hold me back."

It took them four days of hard riding to come across King Hywel of Dyfed, close to his borders. He greeted them warmly, and Wulfstan found himself very confused by the open welcome. Did he not know that they came to do him harm this time? That Wulfstan, the man he'd once rewarded, gripped his dagger in his hand so hard that his knuckles had turned white.

It became apparent quickly that he didn't, and neither it seemed, did the rest of the men that Ælfwine commanded. Wulfstan fought back his anger. Every time he saw a flash of real friendship with Ælfwine, he did something like this, held back vital information and made Wulfstan feel like a fool.

As King Hywel spoke at length about how he planned on punishing Einion of Dyfed, this time, around, Wulfstan pointedly glowered at Ælfwine, so much so that in the end, Ælfwine excused himself from his place beside Hywel at the welcoming feast they were sharing and hissed angrily at Wulfstan.

"What's your problem?"

"Why did you lie to me?"

"I didn't lie to you. I was bloody honest with you, and fucking well lied to everyone else, you daft sod. Now relax, and enjoy yourself. We'll get our chance later and then we can ride for home, and you at least will be happy again. We won't have killed anyone, but King Hywel and Æthelred is right. He bloody deserves it."

"What's he done to deserve to die?" he queried, but Ælfwine was gone, and Wulfstan was left scowling. Perhaps he would make an excellent ealdorman after all. He was certainly learning how to plot and play allies false. And worse. He was learning to command men who owed him their allegiance to do things they didn't care to do.

King Hywel drank well into the night and with each sip he took, Wulfstan's mood soured until he could barely keep himself upright, the contempt he felt for himself was too much to bear on his shoulders. Ælfwine had made it obvious that he was going to be expected to assassinate King Hywel, here, tonight, when he was so far drunk that no one would be surprised if he passed out in a puddle and foolishly drowned. Only Wulfstan suspected it could not be done quite that easily.

Hywel was a strong man, a warrior still, and Wulfstan doubted he'd be killed so incongruously. He'd need to die with a sword in his hand, and probably a sword in his killer as well.

Added to which Wulfstan didn't think of himself as an assassin, hired on the orders of the King to carry out any such task he deemed fit. He'd far rather have met him in battle when the odds weren't so easy, and his death came as the consequence of a real altercation, not something that would have to be lied about.

He assumed this was all Ealdorman Ælfric's doing and it made him wonder about Ælfwine's words from earlier. Surely he already thought that man was on the way out, so why had he decided to fulfil this request. Would it not have been easier to the men, and on his own conscious, if they'd thought of another way to kill the man?

Slowly, the evening wound its way down and by the time Wulfstan was almost beyond himself with fatigue, the only sounds in the great hall they'd met Hywel within were those of people snoring. Only Wulfstan seemed to remain awake, although he was pretending to sleep, and even Ælfwine was snoring at Hywel's side. Wulfstan assumed he didn't sleep, but he wasn't convinced. Maybe even Ælfwine wanted to be able to deny all accountability.

Stealthily, so as not to disturb any of those who slept near him, he worked his way closer and closer to his Lord, checking all the time by the dim light of the embers of the fire whether anyone was still awake or not.

Not that King Hywel didn't have guards. He did, it's just that they were outside the hall and not likely to come inside unless the King called for them. Wulfstan wasn't planning on giving him a chance.

His breath sounded loud in his ear, as did his footsteps, and he almost gasped with shock when Ælfwine's head popped up next to his own, just when he was examining how truly asleep Hywel was. Ælfwine's breath stank of mead and Wulfstan coughed as he inhaled some of his breath.

Ælfwine smirked apologetically.

"I thought it was best if we made sure he was well and truly out for the count."

"My thanks my Lord," Wulfstan uttered sarcastically, and Ælfwine's good humour vanished.

"We need to make it look like an accident. Ælfric doesn't want it to be common knowledge that we killed their King."

"What the fuck?" Wulfstan mouthed. Why go to all this trouble of having the two forces meet if the English wanted complete deniability?

"I only follow orders," Ælfwine muttered into the silence, and Wulfstan felt his eyes rolling upwards in sheer bloody annoyance.

One thing was sure, though, Ælfwine had ensured that Hywel was deeply asleep by plying him with excellent food and even better mead. He was catatonic, even when Wulfstan tried to rouse him, he didn't even hear a grunt of annoyance.

"Do you want to watch?" he asked Ælfwine.

"Not really, but I'm commanding you to do it, so I should see exactly what happens."

With those words, Wulfstan placed one of his hands over the sleeping King's mouth, a piece of cloth scrunched up and ready to gag him, and the other he put over his nose. He then promptly pinched the nose of the man shut and waited for the struggling to begin. He'd never killed a man like this before, but he knew it would work, and it wouldn't leave any marks on him either. Just as Ealdorman Ælfric had ordered, it would look like a tragic accident.

Ælfwine was silent at his side, his head swivelling from side to side as he ensured they weren't being observed, but there was no movement, none at all. Hywel didn't stir from his deep sleep apart from a final jerk, just before his breath stopped and he slumped even further over the table he'd been sleeping against.

Wulfstan was breathing hard, and he felt as though everyone would hear his beating heart, but there was no one awake in the hall, and not even Ælfwine commented on how noisy he was being.

He moved his hands, being careful to remove the gag with them, and he turned to Ælfwine. He felt haunted and soiled by what he'd just done.

Ælfwine placed a hand on his arm and offered him a grim smile.

"Once more we do the bidding of men against our wishes," he said, and Wulfstan nodded numbly.

Ælfwine promptly settled himself down in his chair next to the now dead Hywel and Wulfstan picked his way back through the sleeping bodies to return to his previous position as well. He wanted nothing more than to run from the hall but that would arouse far too much suspicion.

Instead, his breath heavy, he settled himself down to sleep again, and if not to sleep, then to at least give the impression of sleep. It had already been a ridiculously long day, and somehow he thought the night would be even longer.

He was wrong. He slept almost immediately, worn out by his anger and frustration at his actions. He was woken in the morning by a great screech of outrage and the feel of cold iron on his neck. He sighed deeply. Now came the time to lie.

CHAPTER 7 – AD985

The Witan

Wulfstan stepped inside the grand hall at Winchester once more, unsure of his reception and his feelings about where he was and why he was there. He'd not been summoned to account for his actions in the death of King Hywel, in fact far from it. It was almost as though he and Ælfwine had played no part in it. Ealdorman Ælfric, now, he was a man keen to have his name added to any great task that the King asked to be done. Only, all of a sudden, it was not what the King had demanded, and Ealdorman Ælfric was fighting for his survival.

The twisting ways of the Witan weren't welcome to Wulfstan, and although he'd asked Ælfwine if he could attend, he was starting to regret his decision.

Young Leofwine accompanied them, and Wulfstan was happy to have him at his side. But he was stunned by the sudden change in Ælfwine. He was no longer content just to do as he was told but rather, he was bold enough to strike out on his own. Wulfstan didn't think he was setting himself up to succeed Ealdorman Ælfric when he was banished by the Witan, despite what he'd alluded to in Gwynedd, but he was definitely up to something.

The Witan was a changed placed to the last time he'd visited it. Now there were only five ealdormen, soon to be only four as Ælfwine had confided in him, and they were no longer so polarised in opinion. Ealdorman Æthelwine was firmly supported by Ealdorman Brythnoth still, and Æthelweard was a close companion too. All three of the men were staunch supporters of the King. Ealdorman Thored was an unknown to Wulfstan, although he'd been an occasional attendee at the Witan for many years. He was now raised above them all. Then there was, of course, Ealdorman Ælfric, a man who'd held his position only flightingly and who seemed keen to lose it.

The King was still too young, but tall, well muscled and firm in his stance. He seemed steady enough as he walked inside the great hall, his eyes flicking to where his mother might once have sat, but she'd been banished from the Court and rumours abounded that she was being sent to a nunnery and would never appear in public again. Wulfstan still doubted that but time would tell whether he was to be proved correct or not in his approximation of her.

In her place, another now sat, the King's wife. Ælfgifu. A quiet, young woman and the mother of his first son, Athelstan, named after the first King of the English and Æthelred's great uncle. She was the daughter of Ealdorman Thored of Northumbria and that, more than anything, accounted for Thored's presence at the Witan. Wulfstan approved of Æthelred's choice of a wife. In going to Thored, he'd managed to completely sidestep the old rifts that had run through the Witan. At the same time, he'd ensured that his son would always have allies who were family. It was perhaps that, more than anything, that had caused the problems at the beginning of the reign.

The once sprawling family of Edward, son of Alfred the Great, had almost managed to breed itself into obscurity and neither of the children of Edgar, grandson of Edward, had been able to call on family members to ensure their reign should be long and fruitful. Not until now.

The King wasted little time in turning to business, and his business was mostly concerned with Ealdorman Ælfric and his transgressions. It didn't make for pleasant hearing, and the King was determined that all should hear what he had to say.

Ealdorman Ælfric had served the royal family for many years, but it seemed as though and despite his promotion to Ealdorman only two years ago, the King was unhappy with everything he'd ever done. He had manipulated the coinage and gained from its re-striking by not passing on the proceeds to the King. He'd acted outside his remit in dealing with King Hywel of Dyfed. He'd opened a dialogue with the King of the Scots even though the King had forbidden it, preferring to send his father by law to act on his behalf, and he'd made men swear an oath to him that seemed to supersede any promise they owed to the King.

The list went on and on and Wulfstan, despite himself, found himself agreeing with some of the charges. Ealdorman Ælfric had certainly been no Ealdorman Ælfhere. His motivations were difficult to unravel, but it was clear that he felt he'd been waiting in the wings for far too long and should have risen from his rank amongst the men of government many years before he did. He'd long been the lead figure amongst the semi-nobles and felt he should have been rewarded far sooner than he was.

Wulfstan watched the King carefully. He spoke clearly and concisely and without rancour. The charges he laid before the Witan had been carefully composed, and he could tell, just from looking at Ealdorman Ælfric, that he knew he'd not be leaving the Witan with his position intact. He almost wondered why he'd come at all. Wouldn't it have just been better to leave when the King's ire was discovered? But then, there'd be no honour in running away from the allegations. They needed to be faced, even if they were found to be truthful.

When the King had finished speaking, he looked around the room with some interest, waiting to see who would speak out for the disgraced individual. He apparently didn't expect anyone to, but, the men of the Witan were just as honourable as Ealdorman Ælfric after all.

"My Lord," Ealdorman Æthelwine stood slowly as he spoke,

"if I might speak for just a moment in defence of Ealdorman Ælfric."

The King looked at him with some surprise then gestured that he could go ahead. The early morning sun was shining fully on the King as he sat before his assembled Witan and for a moment, he looked resplendent and every inch the perfect King as ordained by God. His clothes flashed with jewels, and his crown had been placed on his head for this very extraordinary meeting.

"My thanks my Lord," Ealdorman Æthelwine spoke quietly, bowing his head towards the King before turning so that he could take in the view of everyone before him and still see the King behind him.

"I will be brief and say only this. Many of the allegations against Ealdorman Ælfric are of a severe nature and have been brought to the attention of the King by more than just one man. And yet I would offer a word of caution and hope it might temper the reaction of everyone within this room. The role of Ealdorman is not an easy one. It is an honour to serve both our King and the people who look to us as a representative of the King, but it also elicits great jealousy from those who lack the same access to the King."

"These allegations are, as I say, serious, and yet, I can't help but wonder if some of the charges have been embellished by the men and women who've made the complaints, almost as though there is someone within this hall who wants Ealdorman Ælfric gone. I would ask those people to carefully consider their actions and the impact they will have on this man's life. If any of those people are truly honourable, I would ask them to step forward and speak out." He paused then and looked around the room.

"Ealdorman Ælfric has been honourable enough to attend the Witan and answer the charges. It would be equally noble if he faced his accuser."

There was some consternation amongst the assembled crowd at the speech, and Wulfstan felt his eyebrows rise in surprise. Of all the things that Ealdorman Æthelwine could have said, he'd not been expecting a call for the honour to be satisfied. Not at all.

Ealdorman Æthelwine paused, as though to allow people to speak out, and King Æthelred scanned the crowd keenly. His face was pensive as he did so. It was evident that he'd not considered the idea of a conspiracy amongst his Witan, and that surprised Wulfstan. After all the years of in-fighting and backstabbing, surely he'd come to realise that these men and women were only that, men and women made from flesh and blood and likely to err as much as any other.

Ealdorman Ælfric was looking at the King too, as though he tried to stop himself from looking at anyone in particular. This was honour at work as well. Ealdorman Ælfric, if he knew who the perpetrators were, was clearly not about to accuse them publicly. If Ealdorman Æthelwine suspected as well, it must be an open secret, a bit like the assassination of King Hywel.

They'd managed to convince King Hywel's men that the death was natural, but as soon as they'd all returned to England, Ealdorman Ælfric had gone out of his way to broadcast the lie inherent in that.

Whoever the perpetrator was, they were not about to make themselves known to the King, and after long moments had passed Ealdorman Æthelwine sighed deeply and bowed his head respectfully to the King. It was evident he was bitterly disappointed.

The King, his eyes still scanning the crowd, finally refocused his eyes on Ealdorman Ælfric, but his gaze was now conflicted. Wulfstan wondered what he'd do now. He squared his shoulders and glanced swiftly to his wife, where she sat, nursing their child in her arms. Wulfstan hadn't noticed the boy before but now he did.

"I'll think on this matter for another day, allow time for any who have further information to bring it to me. For now, we'll move onto other issues."

And so they did, but the day was long and uncomfortable and

every time the conversation at the front of the hall lapsed, whispered conversations sprang up, and they were all concerned with what the Ealdorman had meant when he'd spoken as he had.

Finally, when they were released from their day of discussion and debate, Wulfstan turned to Ælfwine.

"Do you know who Æthelwine meant?"

He'd spent much of the day trying to decide if Ælfwine's renewed interest in the Witan could have anything to do with his involvement in the downfall of Ealdorman Ælfric, but he'd dismissed the idea. Ælfwine wasn't manipulative enough to plot something as complex as that.

"No, I have no idea, and it's unsettling. I thought the King was passed all this factionalism, but it appears as though that's not the case. There's someone who will gain from Ealdorman Ælfric's departure, but as Ealdorman Æthelwine was the one to bring it to everyone's attention, it can't be him. It would be too big a risk to draw attention to the matter if he was to blame. It would be far too risky.

"What of Ealdorman Thored? Would he do it?"

"He should be the least concerned with politics at the Witan. His daughter is the King's wife. There's nothing else for him to do," Ælfwine offered, reaching for and helping himself to more of the roast boar they were being served with.

Wulfstan lapsed into silence. They were within the King's great hall once more, but this time, they were being feted with a huge feast, an indication of the King's largesse to his faithful followers. The ealdormen were liberally scattered around the hall, and they all had men and women coming to them to ask for their intervention or just to gossip about the day's events. Even Ealdorman Ælfric was not short of petitioners, although he might only hold his position for another day.

Wulfstan looked around the room.

"What about Ælfweard or Ælfsige or even Wulfhelm."

They were all high ranking men of Æthelred's government, and sometimes allies of Ælfwine. He only laughed at Wulfstan, his face creasing slightly as he ate.

"Honestly Wulfstan, Ealdorman Æthelwine might just have been trying to lessen the blow, there might not be anyone who's trying to have Ealdorman Ælfric banished."

"You could be right, I suppose, but I don't think that Æthelwine would have spoken unless he knew something."

"Well unless he chooses to share it with us, I don't believe that we're ever going to know."

Wulfstan nodded as he ate. Ælfwine was probably right. Still, he couldn't stop himself from running scenarios through his head. He kept it to himself when he started to examine the King's motifs. Ælfwine didn't like it when he spoke out about his fears about the King.

There was a minor disturbance at the door, and he turned with surprise to see the King's mother entering the feast. The King looked at her once and then away and made no move to have her ejected from the feast. Clearly, the rumours of the rift with her son had been exaggerated.

She walked confidently and quickly made her way towards the King's wife. She wasn't sat beside the King, but rather at a smaller table where she could nurse her son when he needed it. Wulfstan had thought it a little odd when he first saw her there, and the look of fury that swept over her face when she laid eyes on the Lady Elfrida was all Wulfstan needed to see. The anointed Queen, the King's mother, was usurping the King's wife, a woman who the King didn't intend to be his Queen.

He watched her fuss over the baby, calling for more blankets and undermining Ælfgifu's every action and he decided he was probably looking in the wrong place for any miscreant. The most likely candidate for the current unease within the Witan was the old Queen. But why eluded him.

Despite Ealdorman Æthelwine's words the previous day, and the King's apparent intent to wait and see if the allegations against Ælfric could be disproved, no one came forward the next day, and Ealdorman Ælfric was officially banished from the realm of England. Wulfstan felt a brief flare of pity for the man, especially when he took the time to bid farewell to Ælfwine and himself, and as he watched him ride away back to his lands, and from there to wherever he was going to seek sanctuary, Wulfstan considered what forces were at play. It seemed as though King Æthelred's reign was beset with problems. He only hoped the King would be able to surmount them all. One day.

CHAPTER 8 – AD986

Near Deerhurst

T he cross was heavy in his hand. He'd come to realize that it weighed him down with its memories and with the attendant guilt that infected him whenever he glanced at the piece.

Ælfwine had called him a fool, but he didn't much care. His Lord had endowed the church at Deerhurst, giving as much of his wealth as he could afford to ensure that it stood as a lasting testament to his position. It was now five hides richer in land and Wulfstan also planned to gift the cross to him so that he could in turn gift it the Abbot and his church.

He didn't want the cross. It was a stain on his honour that he struggled to reconcile with who he wanted to be. It would be better for him if it adorned a church rather than the interior of his war chest and worse, that burned itself into his heart whenever he happened upon it.

There was currently no ealdorman of Mercia to come to the church for its rededication, but that wasn't stopping Ælfwine from going ahead with his intentions. He was no ealdorman, and neither did he want to be one, but in their local community he was important, and on occasion, he had been known to have the ear of the King. He'd served two ealdormen and knew much of what was expected of one. If the King sometimes sent to him and asked him to ensure tasks were completed and justice served, Ælfwine, still confident of his abilities, was happy to comply.

It didn't make him an ealdorman, but the general population didn't seem to make that distinction.

Leofwine and the rest of the household had made the short journey to the church at Deerhurst and Wulfstan felt it was a good day to rededicate the small church. The sun was warm and gentle, a breeze flowed now and then, and a cacophony of animal noises ceased on their arrival. It was early summer, and lambs were in the fields, and the birds were busy with their hatchlings. It forced a smile onto Wulfstan's face despite his best intentions.

"Wulfstan," Leofwine called his name, and he found himself going towards the boy. Wulfstan had the distinct impression that Leofwine had been staying away from him since the events of last year, but he didn't know whether it was out of respect for him or whether he now feared him.

"Leofwine?" Wulfstan asked, and the boy's eyes lit up a little.

"I know the timing's not the best but, well, do you remember when we went to Winchester?" Wulfstan remembered far too well and hoped the boy wasn't about to ask him about it. "Well, I asked you about how many men you'd killed, and you wouldn't tell me."

Wulfstan was nodding now. He had an idea of where the conversation was going.

"I do, Leofwine, yes. Why?"

"Well," and the boy considered his next words, while Wulfstan waited patiently to see if what he thought was about to happen, really would.

"Can you teach me?"

The tone was plaintive, and Wulfstan was relieved at the question. He was pleased it wasn't about the King.

"Your father teaches you?" he said, and Leofwine's face clouded a little.

"He teaches me how to fight honourably. I want to know all

the sneaky moves that can save your life when you're in a tight spot."

"Ah," Wulfstan said. He'd thought this moment would come sooner or later, and it irked him a little. Ælfwine might be the more noble man in battle, but where politics were concerned, he fought dirty. Not Wulfstan, oh no, he only fought dirty when he was on the battlefield, and only then if he had to and yet that was what the lad saw when he looked at him.

"You think it'll be necessary to learn to fight in such a way then?"

Leofwine did him the courtesy of considering his answer.

"The King doesn't like me for my encounter with him when I was a child. And the Vikings. Well, I don't think they're going to stop. Do you?"

Wulfstan was impressed by the lad's logic. He shared his views on the Vikings. He didn't think they were going to stop. Every year, without fail, there was another raid, and rumours were rife that it wasn't only England under attack. The lands of Gwynedd and Dyfed have also come under attack. He wondered what was happening in the land of the Scots. He doubted they were immune to attacks.

It seemed as though Leofwine was more far-sighted than even his father, and the King as well.

"I'll teach you. But we'll check your father doesn't have any real issues with it first. It's honourable to check with him."

Leofwine's face flickered quickly from joy to annoyance, but he nodded all the same.

"My thanks, Wulfstan. I'll ask him. I wouldn't want him to think that it was your idea."

"Very good Leofwine. Your honour does you proud."

"I wish it did more than that, but thank you all the same."

Leofwine paused then and took a deep breath. The church at Deerhurst was upon them. His face was difficult to read. There was clearly something about this place that he didn't much like.

"It smells of death," he said, and Wulfstan startled at the words, but he couldn't reply because Leofwine had already walked inside.

How could Leofwine know what death smelt like? He'd never even encountered death before. It was a strange thing to say, and it occupied Wulfstan's mind during the entire service, so much so that in the end, he had to approach Leofwine and ask him what it all meant.

Leofwine's eyes were a little hooded as he listened to Wulfstan's rambling question but he was patient and clearly intended to answer.

"I've always thought it," he said when Wulfstan had stopped stumbling over his words to reach the crux of the conversation. "There's something here, or there will be something here, of great importance to my family and me, and it worries me. Sometimes I dream about it, and sometimes I don't, but I've always thought the same, ever since I was a small boy."

"Your mother isn't buried here. She had died before you moved to Deerhurst."

"I know, and it's not her. It's something else."

With that, the boy walked away, but the boy's words disturbed Wulfstan. He'd thought the lad was above believing in strange portents. Clearly, he was wrong.

CHAPTER 9 – AD989

The Land of the Hwicce

Wulfstan allowed his horse to go where it wanted. He was in no particular rush on such a fine summer's day. Life had slowed down to a mere walking pace, and he was happy to enjoy it. It had been a long hard few years, but he now felt as though Ælfwine was nearing his destination and might soon have what he desired at his fingertips.

Wulfstan was pleased for him.

It might have taken over ten years but Leofwine, grown to almost a man now, had finally been allowed to attend upon the King at his Court. The word fostering might have been used, but actually, Leofwine was gone as a companion for the King, just as the King's mother, the Lady Elfrida had always intended, only it had been done on terms that Ælfwine was happier with.

He'd decided he never needed to remarry and was content at his home in Deerhurst although more often than not he rode out and acted for the King in the wider Mercian realms. There was no longer an official Ealdorman of Mercia, but Wulfstan was sure it wouldn't be much longer in coming. As soon as King Æthelred learned to assert himself once more, and managed to rid himself of yet another overbearing ealdorman, Wulfstan was convinced he'd make the announcement regarding Ælfwine.

But for now, he didn't care either way. After eleven long years, he was coming home, to see his wife and his sons. No sooner had Ælfwine dispatched Leofwine to the royal court than he'd begun to impress on his friend that he too needed to make some necessary changes in his life, and if those led him back to his wife and his sons, then he would be happy to release him from his commendatory vow.

Wulfstan had bickered and argued his way through the early summer, more than anything because he'd wanted to believe it could be true. Events with King Hywel of Gwynedd had soured him. The frequent small-scale Viking raids kept him on his toes, but really, he was a simple man, and he wanted a simple life.

He'd not sent any word to his wife of his intentions, but he knew better than to. If he'd let her know he was coming, she could just as easily have sent word to him to tell not to and after eleven years, he thought he deserved a second chance. Or rather, a second, second chance.

He'd not beaten this path once in the intervening years. He'd made his promise when he'd left and despite everything that she might say about him, he'd not broken his word. Not once. No matter the times he'd ached to see his sons, to hold them in his arms, he'd let her have her way. It had perhaps been easier not to see them at all than torture himself with what he was missing out on.

His once family home was located on good farmland, not more than a day's ride from Deerhurst. In his first few months away from home, the closeness of his sons had tormented him every day. Now though he only found it ironic that he could step so quickly from being Ælfwine's highly regarded commander, to nothing more than a humble farmer so fast.

His horse took him home, despite the fact the beast had not made the journey in eleven years either. Its head was down, and he felt that the animal, known just as Midnight, was as twisted with confusion and indecision as he was. Still, he was glad he had him with him to make the steps for him. At least that way he knew he'd make it home.

He walked through a thick forest, a track laid out carefully so that none would stray, and he remembered the time he'd laboured to bring the path into existence. He'd been genuinely worried that his wife or his children would get lost and never make their way home again. He needn't have worried. It was only ever he who'd struggled.

The path before him was lit with deep summer greens and the pungent smell of the forest floor. The horse almost bounded from side to side because the trail was so spongy underfoot. He breathed in deeply of the smell of home. Why had he ever left?

Emerging abruptly from the protection of the forest canopy, he raised his arm to shield his eyes from the blinding light. The smell of fire reached his nostrils, but it was some time before he could focus on the home he'd built with his bare hands, while his wife sat by, heavily pregnant and watched him. But that had been before ....

The house was well maintained, and some fresher timbers had been added to support those that had rotted. He'd always thought it likely that the post closest to him would rot the soonest. For some reason the ground there had always been wet. He'd cursed his ill luck when he'd realised that he'd not correctly surveyed the ground before starting the build. But by then it had been too late, the option to spend months and months more of living under a canvas roof or build the house where it was had been no choice at all. He hoped his sons hadn't laboured too long and hard to replace the timber.

His horse made his way over to the water trough and drank deeply of the cold fluid, making it clear he was going no further. If he hadn't been quite so nervous, he might well have enjoyed the stubbornness of his horse and his obvious happiness at being home. There were no other horses that Wulfstan could see and he hoped that meant his sons were busy at their work. It would make it easier for everyone if he saw his wife alone for the first time.

He'd barely jumped from his horse when he felt inquisitive eyes on him. He looked up and met the dark hazel eyes of his wife. He gasped in recognition, and he stilled, wondering what she'd do next.

"You're back then?" she said, turning to walk back towards the entrance to their home. Of all the responses he'd been expecting, that wasn't one of them.

"Did you miss me?" he asked, following her quickly. She seemed almost happy to see him.

"Of course I did, you fool, but it's only been a few days, so I survived. The boys kept me busy."

His heart sank then. It was evident she wasn't in the here and now. He wondered why he'd expected her to be. She walked inside the hall he'd built, and he stood outside, uncertain of himself. Should he go inside, or should he just leave again?

The view of her was tantalising, arousing emotions and desires in him that he'd long since thought extinguished and he didn't want to be tempted. He didn't want to be accused of taking advantage of her. He stood, and he worried, and finally she came back outside.

"Are you not coming in Wulfstan? Dinner is almost ready, and I've laid you a place. The boys will be a while longer yet. They're down in the distant meadow seeing to some sheep."

Her eyes were open and honest, no hint of her past aggression touched her face, and her beauty swayed him. Perhaps it would be okay just to share a meal with her. Nothing more.

Inside the hall, he could see where his sons had filled the vast space with their possessions. There were some bows and many arrows along one wall and along another, there was a collection of skulls that must have come either from sheep or prized hounds. He didn't know either way.

There was a small fire blazing in the central hearth and to the side of it a small workstation that held bowls of herbs and some vegetables as well as a deadly looking knife.

Behind the hearth was a slightly raised table, the wood had come from discarded remnants when he'd built the hall, and along its length, he could see deep grooves where his sons had sat down to eat. He placed his weapons carefully beside the open doorway and went to sit in his usual place. His wife didn't bat an eyelid as he did so but continued to speak to him as though he'd been gone a day or two and not for eleven years.

"There's a hole in the fencing around the garden, and I think some animal or other is helping itself to my best vegetables and herbs. I've asked the boys to fix it, but they ignore me. If you get a chance, could you see to it for me? There's no rush." She added when he went to stand on hearing her words. In the past, she would have berated him until his job was done. Now, though, things seem different, calmer.

She placed a bowl of mutton stew before him and placed some flatbreads besides his hand. The bowl was one of many he'd fashioned himself from weathered wood, and he was surprised by the sudden lump that formed in his throat on seeing it. It was as though he'd walked backwards in time when he'd led his horse through the forest and back into the daylight.

As she did so, her hand brushed against his, and a thrill of pleasure shot up his arm. His breath caught in his throat, and he looked away from her, focusing on anything apart from the sight of her. Her beauty had been his greatest undoing.

She softly laughed as she sat beside him.

"It's good to know I still have that effect on you," and she tucked into her food.

It tasted good. Nothing as fancy as he might eat when he was attending upon the King but that didn't bother him. This tasted far better because it tasted of home.

"I want to thank you," she said, and Wulfstan looked at her now, noticing the stray wrinkle around her eyes, and the way her hair seemed to have greyed a little in places. Clearly, time had passed for her as well as it had for him at Deerhurst, despite appearances to the contrary.

"For what?" he asked, as he spooned his stew into his mouth.

"I asked a hard thing of you. Or rather I demanded it, and I never gave you the opportunity not to do it, and yet you went, and you respected my wishes. I thank you for that."

Suddenly she seemed to be back with him, and he wondered when the change had taken place within her mind.

"It's not been easy. I can't deny that. But you're my wife, and I honour you."

"The boys have missed you," she continued, as though he hadn't spoken, "and there have been times when I thought the punishment too severe. But every time, I've held firm in my resolve, even when the boys begged me to send for you."

Wulfstan didn't speak. It pained him to know that his sons had wanted him and their mother had denied them their request.

"You'd be proud of them. They look like you, and think like you, although they don't have your skill with a sword because I never let them learn. They know how to raise sheep and cattle, grow crops and tend to the ills that might befall a prosperous farmhouse. They'll make better husbands because of it."

"I'm proud of you for raising them so well," he finally managed to say, even though the words felt empty to him. He'd wanted his boys to have choices, just as he'd had, he'd not wanted them to become farmers if they'd wanted to be monks or warriors.

"Will you stay and see them?" she asked, and Wulfstan felt disconcerted by the always changing tenor of the conversation. One moment it was as though he'd never left and would be staying forever, and the next it was acknowledged that he was merely visiting and would be gone again soon. He wanted to stay, especially now he'd seen his home made flesh again, and not just in his memories.

He'd built this place with his bare hands, for his wife and his children and he wanted nothing more than to kick aside his shield and sword and stay home and raise sheep and cattle.

"Yes, I'll wait and see the boys," he answered, aware she was waiting for a reply.

"Good," she said, and having finished her meal, she began to tidy away her own and Wulfstan's bowl. As she did so, she leant over him, and her fragrance assaulted him, and he found himself reaching for her hand and holding it tenderly in his own as she smiled at him.

"You still have soft hands. How do you keep them so soft?" she joked, placing the bowls carefully back onto the table and folding herself into his lap. Wulfstan held so still he almost thought he might have stopped breathing. What was she doing?

Reaching out with her free hand, she ran it over his face, her skin a little jagged against his own but still leaving a burning scorch mark in its path. It had been a very long time since he'd last been with a woman.

"Your face is as I remember it, although a little too pale. Don't you spend as much time in the sun as you used to?"

She didn't wait for him to reply, but bent her head towards his lips, touching them gently with her own. He felt his desire burning inside him and he desperately looked around, hoping that somehow his sons would be home and would put an end to this strange little scenario. What was he supposed to do? Kiss her and bed her as he used to do?

Her tongue tickled the inside of his mouth as he tried to maintain his equilibrium but when her hands began to trace his face and his neck, his stomach and his back, he found himself caught up in his emotions. He kissed her back then, passionately and for so long that he almost forgot how to breathe. She returned the kiss, and it deepened, became insistent, demanding, craving far more than one kiss can ever give.

Still trying to stay calm and lucid, he pulled a little away from her, but she groaned at him and pulled him closer, before forcing him backwards so that he lay on the raised wooden floor, and she straddled him from side to side. She was breathing just as heavily as he was now, and he allowed her to continue to set the pace of events.

She pulled at his tunic and worked it free so that she could run her warm hands over his superheated skin and he gasped in pleasure when her fingers worked their way a little lower and began work on his leggings.

He grabbed her hands then, taking them in his own, and her eyes met his with frustration. He gazed into her beautiful face, taking the time to memorise how she looked now so that he'd not forget what it was like to be desired once more by the woman he'd always loved.

She smiled at him, a slow smile that spread across her face with delight and she wormed her hands out of his and returned to her task.

He worked his way upwards, liberally leaving kisses all over her shoulders, the only part of her body he could reach, and then he shuffled on the floor, and he felt his leggings come loose, and warm hands on the tops of his legs. A delighted chuckle erupted from her mouth, and he found himself being swept along by her wants and needs, no thought of the future.

He felt warm skin on his legs and then hot kisses on his face. She straddled him, and he gasped with pleasure, and all thoughts of anything other than the here and now evaporated from his mind.

He was home, and he was with the woman he loved.

The fire burnt low as they reunited and he didn't care at all, not until he felt a blast of chill air on his skin and looked up from his doze to see the eyes of his sons looking at him in shock.

He giggled in embarrassment, reaching for his clothes and his eldest son met his eyes and grinned with delight, all traces of worry and fear instantly erased when he recognised the man who'd just slept with his mother.

At his side, his wife snored loudly, and the three of them burst out laughing at the noise, all trying to stifle the noise so that they wouldn't wake her. He waved his hand at them both, and they walked outside, and he staggered as silently as he could to his feet and went outside to be reunited with his sons.

They were waiting for him twenty steps away from the hall, they were looking outwards, at their farm land but he could tell they were excited by the childhood tells he'd always smirked about. The elder liked to juggle from one foot to another, and the younger washed his hands one inside the other.

"Boys," he called, and they turned to look at him. They were still grinning, and he embraced them both, surprised when his arms didn't reach all the way around them, as they once had. The passage of years surprised him once more.

"I came to visit you," he began, and they shushed him.

"She has some good days and some bad days. She might not ..." the elder looked to the younger as though looking for the right word, "be the same when she wakes."

He felt his heart tug at the news, but he tried to mask it as well as he could.

"I didn't expect to be welcomed at all. I'm ... I'm happy that she wanted to see me."

"She more than wanted to see you," his younger son chuckled, and Wulfstan slapped him on the back.

"Stop talking about your mother, now tell me, everything about you. I've missed you."

They began to talk, the years flowing over him as he heard every little detail that his sons decided to share with him. His sadness at missing so much disappeared. His boys were generous with their forgiveness and their time, sharing everything they could, and telling stories about each other. They laughed and chuckled, and Wulfstan almost felt the stain of his murder of Hywel lift from his shoulders.

Almost, until he heard the voice of his wife, calling from the hall. She sounded angry, and he swallowed against his sudden fear. He stood and turned to face her, wondering what he'd see, but she simply waved at him, and he relaxed.

She was still herself.

"Come on father. She'll cook dinner for us, and she'll stay as she is. Tomorrow might be different, but we've learnt to enjoy it while we can."

He nodded as he watched her turn to go back into their hall, her hair falling loosely down her back. She was a beautiful woman. There was no denying it. It was such a pity that her illness had robbed her of her ability to remember where she was, and who she was, at least some of the time.

Inside the hall, he glanced back towards where only that afternoon he'd lain with his wife. His face flushed a little, and his elder son grinned at him when he saw where he looked. He ignored the look and went to stand beside his wife. He wasn't sure how long she'd been awake for, but there was another meal ready, and his stomach rumbled loudly.

"You always had the appetite of three men," she joked, and he relaxed his slightly tense posture. He'd been worried, despite the reassurance of his sons, that she'd change her mind and banish him before he could enter the hall.

That night they drank and ate and talked about life's little things, with no reference to the past or the future, almost as though all that mattered was the present. His sons, Wulf and Wulfhelm, were excellent company, and his wife, Wulflæd, well she'd always been witty when she spoke, and she didn't disappoint that night either.

They told jokes and laughed at each other, and Wulfstan, despite himself, started to hope just a little that his dream might prove to be possible.

When they finally slept, the room swaying quite alarmingly for Wulfstan, he held his wife tight in his arms, and she nestled against him, this time within their bed, surrounded by layers and layers of furs although it was too warm to need them all.

He closed his eyes to the soft breathing of his wife, and he could have sworn he heard the words, 'I love you," leave her lips.

He smiled with joy.

The morning came, and he opened his eyes against the blaze of sunlight from the open doorway as he tried to remember where he was, and then, once he had remembered where he was he panicked. What if his wife had returned to one of her angry personas?

He needn't have worried. His wife was busily preparing breakfast and issuing instructions to her sons on what needed doing that day. When he joined them, rubbing his head a little ruefully, the boys nudged each other and grinned. There was far too much knowledge in that grin.

His wife swept him a look, her face a little stern and he braced himself for an angry tirade.

"You can help the boys in the far field. You could teach them a few things about how you repair hedges and fences."

His sons looked outraged, but he was pleased to be put to work doing something so mundane. It would suit his tender head to be out working in the sunshine.

"What will you be doing today?" he asked his wife, but she only glared even more sternly at him, and he knew better than to ask. She'd always had her way of getting important tasks done, some of them he knew were not particularly conventional, part of the reason her reputation suffered, but he knew better than to press the point. He would get to spend another day with his sons. That was all that mattered. If tonight, when they returned to the family hall, she'd changed again, he would ride away far more contented than he had been for ten years.

He didn't get a day or even two, but ten and he enjoyed every single one of them, he and his sons relaxing around each other and his wife pleased to have him around and in her bed. He'd almost convinced himself he could stay but then, on the tenth day, when he and his sons returned home from the farm, his measly possessions were waiting for him outside the hall door, and his horse was saddled.

He was hot and sweaty from his day's work, but he knew better than to force the issue. It was his elder son who pointed out the problem and he detained him before he could go inside the house.

"It'll be best if you don't," Wulf said, his hand firm on his father's shoulder. His steps faltered, and he looked where his son did, and his heart sank a little. This time, he'd go more honourably than when his sons had been young boys.

"What will you do?" he asked them both, seeing his sorrow mirrored in their eyes.

"We have alternative beds in the barn with the animals. We've some food stored there as well, so we'll spend the night, and maybe the next few days there. It'll pass soon."

Wulfhelm was looking at his home with a twisted face and Wulfstan almost admonished the boy but then he spoke, his voice hopeful and Wulfstan felt pain rip through him.

"You could stay with us. See if she recovers and allows you to stay."

Wulfstan knew it didn't work like that. Somehow, after all these years, he'd managed to return during one of her more lucid moments. He was aware that it could be months before she was back to herself again. It was clear that Wulf knew that as well, but he was a little older than his brother, and Wulfstan had learned during the last ten days, far more grounded than his brother who was prone to flights of fancy.

"No, Wulfhelm, it'll be best if father goes. She might be like this for weeks or even months."

The lad's shoulders slumped, and Wulfstan reached out and grabbed him in a huge embrace.

"Look, you're older now, wiser than when I first left. You'll be able to seek me out if you need me now, I'm only at Deerhurst, and I can come if there's a problem. I don't want to have her turn her ire on you as well as me. Your brother's right. It'll be best if I leave now."

He could feel his son shaking in his arms, and at that moment he'd have done anything to stay. Anything to know that his children weren't torn between loyalty to their mother and her strange mood swings, and their father and his absenteeism.

"I know all that, but well, it would be better if you stayed."

"You've not needed me these last few years, despite what your mother might have said over the last few days. The farm is fantastic and will be yours when your mother is no longer here."

"Why do you accept it so readily?" Wulf asked, voicing a question Wulfstan hadn't ever really liked to answer himself.

"I blame myself for what happened to her. I should have been here when you were born Wulf, then maybe the madness wouldn't have descended on her, and maybe I'd have realised what was happening, but I was only a little older than you two are now, and I had no idea that this sort of thing could even occur."

"I don't think it would have made any difference if you'd been here or not," Wulfhelm said, and Wulfstan glanced at him in surprise.

"Sometimes we have to get the herb woman here to tend to her when she's very low or ill. She won't let us anywhere near her. The herb woman, she explained it all to us. She said it was a tragedy and relatively rare, but that it happened all the same. She said, well, she wasn't entirely begrudging of the way you've dealt with it all."

Wulfstan had never heard a more backhanded compliment, but he accepted it as one anyway. He'd spoken to the herb woman himself on many occasions when he'd still lived within the hall before he'd returned to Ælfwine's war band.

"Will you be alright?" he asked his sons, hoping they'd nod and remove the trace of remorse on their faces.

"Yes, we always are," Wulf offered, smiling a little crookedly at his father.

"Come again, but not within the next year. She'll probably be like this again this time next year. If you want, I could send word to you."

Wulfstan thought about that. Could he spend all year hoping that his wife would love him one more time? He wasn't sure if he could open himself up to the possibility of rebuttal in a year, and then maybe again, the year after. But his sons were both looking at him hopefully.

"Yes, I'll try and do that," he finally said, "and send word if it happens sooner."

The joy on the boy's faces cost him dearly, but he had no choice. With a rough hug and a kiss for them both, which they both rubbed from their faces with disgust, he went to pick up his possessions. They had at least been neatly packed.

He hesitated by the doorway. She must have heard their exchange, and he would have liked nothing better than to see her one more time, but he knew better.

With a wave for his son's that masked his deep despair, he

returned to his horse, which met him with a sharp head butt to the back for having ignored him for much of the last ten days and mounted up. As he rode out of the sun-dappled glen and into the overcast forest, he mourned the life he could simply never have.

PART 2

CHAPTER 10 – AD991

Deerhurst

T he news from East Anglia was poor. Everyone in the hall
recognised it for what it was, although no one spoke just
yet.

The Vikings had come, as Leofwine had said they would on
that fateful day at Deerhurst, and now they had a duty to carry
out. They had to muster and answer the call to arms that had
come from Ealdorman Brythnoth. Unlike the previous two ealdormen of Mercia, he'd never yet called upon Ælfwine's familial
links. But that had changed in a heartbeat. Wulfstan supposed
that a host of armed men, intent on murdering your people
would do that to even the staidest of Ealdormen.

Neither was Brythnoth particularly young. He was an old
man with grandchildren at his knees. He had much to lose if
the Vikings gained a foothold in England. Just as much as every
other man, woman and child who'd been unfortunate enough to
become ensnarled in the attack.

Leofwine, only just returned from his fosterage with the King
was sitting beside his father, his expression pensive. Wulfstan
could already see the danger signs there. The father and son
were on a collision course, and he didn't know who would win,
although he had a relatively good idea.

Brythnoth had called on Ælfwine to mass near to London

with as many men as he could bring. Ælfwine was only the commander of a small force, but the men and their wives within the hall knew that they would all be called upon to do their part. This was what they trained for. This was what all those practice runs against far smaller raiding parties had been for.

Wulfstan knew that some of these men would not return home alive. He hoped he would, but not at the expense of his Lord. He could only live if his Lord did, and they banished the Vikings from their land.

Ælfwine finally stood, his movements slow and measured. He wanted to present himself as a man of reason and forethought, not one who jumped to do the bidding of anyone who asked him. He knew that now, but it had been a lesson that had taken too long to learn.

"Ealdorman Brythnoth, as many of you know, is a relative of mine. Distant, but a relative all the same and when he calls on me and asks me to honour my family ties, I have no choice but to go."

His voice was strong, and yet his eyes held something else, and Wulfstan wasn't sure what it was.

"Yet Ealdorman Brythnoth has no claims to the rest of you, and neither do I."

A chorus of denial was building, but Ælfwine ignored it.

"I'll think nothing less of any of you if you choose not to come. The decision will be your own, and I want you to consider it carefully. This will be a bloody battle. And possibly a decisive one as well. Only come if you know you're prepared for the worst. We will assemble tomorrow at first light and ride to join with Brythnoth. Or at least I will. The rest of you can choose as you will."

Wulfstan grinned a little at Ælfwine. He'd chosen well when he made that speech, but as he sat back down, he saw Leofwine open his mouth to argue, and Wulfstan decided to interject and stop the looming showdown.

"They'll all come anyway," he said, striding towards Ælfwine, for all that he spoke quietly. "But you did the right thing by making them think they have a choice."

Leofwine stopped with his mouth open; his words were unspoken on his lips as he looked from Wulfstan to his father. His eyes narrowed a little, and Wulfstan nodded to show that, yes, he was trying to prevent them from arguing. It had not been easy on either of them since Leofwine had returned from the Court, with ideas of his own and contrary to his father.

Ælfwine looked pensively at Wulfstan.

"They do have a choice. And I want them to take it."

"I know that, but in giving them a choice, you've commanded them just as thoroughly as if you'd given them no choice."

Ælfwine opened his mouth to speak, but Wulfstan interjected.

"It's not your fault. You couldn't have done anything differently. But now, you two must discuss the future and what will happen to this place if we don't return."

Leofwine, his face flushed, managed to speak then.

"I want to come. I demand to come."

Wulfstan smacked the lad on the back.

"I know that Leofwine, and so does your father. But you're not to come. It's not possible. You're the heir, you stay here and keep the place safe from the ravages of other men, should your father fall in battle."

"I'm the better warrior," the youth persisted, and Ælfwine tried to diffuse the situation by laughing. A dangerous tactic but one he tried, all the same, causing Wulfstan to wince.

"I'm the better warrior or even Wulfstan is the better warrior. But not you son. You've never fought in an actual battle. Those games you've played with the King's household troops are nothing compared to a real fight."

"Then I demand to be allowed to take part in a real battle."

"No," Ælfwine said, and for once Wulfstan mirrored his sentiments. If the reports from East Anglia and London were correct, this coming engagement would be nothing for an untried youth to take part in.

Leofwine glared hotly at the two men and turned to walk

away. Ælfwine restrained him with a hand on his shoulder.

"Wulfstan's right. We need to talk about the future."

Leofwine searched his father's face for some clue that he didn't mean the words he was saying, and then he spoke, his voice breaking as he did so.

"But you, you can't die."

"I am as mortal as other men. I can die and one day I will. I hope not yet, but it's better to be prepared."

Leofwine slumped then, his defiance leaving his body.

"Fine, we'll talk then but father, if you go and get yourself bloody killed, I'll never forgive you," he said, his voice hot and rough with emotion.

Ælfwine clasped his son firmly in his strong arms.

"I know that lad. I know."

The next morning Wulfstan had imagined there would be a quiet send off as the men and women took leave of each other. What he'd not expected was to see Leofwine mounted on his horse, with all the accoutrements of battle ready and secured on his horse. Ælfwine's face when he saw his son was one of total outrage.

"Get off that fucking horse," he shouted at Leofwine, not caring who saw or heard their exchange.

Wulfstan admired Leofwine in that instant. He stayed his ground and met his father's angry gaze evenly.

"I've thought long and hard about this, and while I agree in general with what we discussed last night, and while I figured I was happy to stay at home, I find your logic flawed. I should be riding with the men. You gave us all a choice, and I'm exercising my rights."

"I gave my commended men and warriors the option, not you, you dull-witted idiot," his father roared and at that moment something flashed over Ælfwine's face. Wulfstan rushed forward to intervene, but he was too late to prevent Ælfwine from reaching up and grabbing Leofwine and forcing him from his horse.

"I'm your father, and you will do as you're bloody well told. Now get inside."

Ælfwine's face was puce with rage and Wulfstan found himself slowing perceptibly as he neared his oldest friend. Now was not the time to intervene.

"I'm no longer a boy to be kept close and shielded from the world. I know what battle means, and I intend to face the enemy. I'm not about to run away and hide from this."

"I'm not asking you to run away and hide, I'm asking you, as your father, to stay here, keep Deerhurst safe for me to return to. I've worked all my life for this bloody hall and to ensure the safety of you and the rest of my people. I want to ride away knowing that I've accomplished something in this life that might have some permanence, something that might mark me for future generations to sing and talk about."

Leofwine glared at his father, refusing to be swayed by his words, and then Wulfstan's heart sank into his boots.

"You have me, father. You made me, father. Be a little proud of that, why don't you?"

With that, Leofwine angrily removed his possessions from the back of his horse and stormed back into the hall, carefully avoiding every animal, small child and sobbing woman that stood in his way.

Ælfwine glared angrily at his son and then did something else that filled Wulfstan with fear. He mounted his horse, signalled for his men to ride on, and never looked back. Not once.

CHAPTER 11 – AD991

Homecoming

T he heat was sapping any strength he had left. He'd planned on riding all night so that he could impart his devastating news as soon as possible to the recipient of the sad tidings, but now, with the high heat from the bright summer's day, he felt his resolve slipping.

He needed to eat and sleep and recover from the battle. But he also knew that he was dragging his feet, trying to find any way that he could delay the inevitable. He chided himself for his selfishness but couldn't make himself speed his flagging beast, almost as if whilst the news was his own it wasn't quite real, hadn't really happened.

He'd barely closed his eyes all night but every time he'd nodded off in the saddle he's been greeted with a view of his Lord in battle, the battle playing itself out in slow motion behind his closed eyelids in a dazzling array of bright colours and harsh cries. He'd gasped awake time and time again, fighting the nightmare that threatened to drag him down and he warred with himself now. He needed to sleep, but he didn't want to close his eyes again. Never.

And then anger flooded his body. How dare his Lord ask this of him? How dare he be forced to be the one who would have to return alive and face the anger of his Lord's son. No doubt he'd angrily ask him why he lived in place of his father. And Wulfstan wasn't sure he had an answer to that. What he'd understood in the heat of the battle now seemed to make little sense to him. The honour his Lord had wanted to claim for himself and his son by association was as nothing as the dawn light had stolen over the land and Wulfstan had finally comprehended that he'd never see his friend again.

The task was too great a burden, too much for one man, unwelcome and an honour all combined into one. Ælfwine had tasked him with raising his son, almost a man now but with a few minor areas where he still needed to grow, gain confidence and be assured in his own abilities. He was honoured and angry again about it all.

He had his own family, his own wife, and his own sons. And then reining his horse abruptly in, wiping the dusty sweat from his brow, he laughed bitterly at himself. He might well have a wife, but she little regarded him and he'd lived as a bachelor for more years than as a married man. His sons were older than Leofwine, making their own way in the world. He was not needed. Not by any of them. After his ten days with his family two years ago, he'd never yet managed a repeat, although he'd visited. Each and every time he'd been firmly rebuffed and chased from the hall he'd built.

He should have died on the battlefield, not Ælfwine.

The horse, Heard, shifted beneath him. He was as tired and upset as his rider.

With a gentle nudge, he told his horse to walk on, the home of his Lord coming into view in the heat haze that enveloped the land. The neat and tidy main building, the subsidiary buildings now bulging with the harvest, and the gentle curve of the river within which the house nestled.

It was a beautiful home. One he was grateful he lived within.

He sighed deeply.

There was nothing for it.

He needed to see his Lord's son, impart the news of the catastrophe and let the lad come to terms with what had happened.

He knew the news would be very harshly taken. Ælfwine and Leofwine had parted on bad terms and this would destroy the boy.

The horse grew a little more keen beneath him as he realized he was so nearly home, and Wulfstan didn't blame the beast for bringing him home more quickly than he'd have liked. If it wasn't for the burden he wore like a deep winter cloak, he too would have been keen to be home, to see his own bed and eat good food.

Walking through the open gateway Wulfstan shook his head at the irony of finding the house open and welcoming to all, whereas at the eastern coast every one was hunkered down against the onslaught of the huge raiding army and their lightening fast ships, filled with men skilled only at delivering death.

At the gate, the men who were training in the sunbaked yard turned to watch him, their eyes suddenly solemn, and all enjoyment in the day quickly forgotten. They knew what Wulfstan's solitary appearance portended.

Wulfstan didn't see Leofwine amongst them, and slid from his horse slowly, feeling a hundred years old. The horse was taken from him, and he took a breath, squared his shoulders and walked into the welcoming dim glow of his home, his Lord's home and his eyes sought and found Leofwine, and that was all he needed to do.

A beat, two at the most, and Leofwine too realized what Wulfstan's solitary appearance meant. He slumped to his seat; his face grey and old and Wulfstan felt renewed grief smother him.

He couldn't do this.

He wasn't strong enough.

But he would.

He knelt before the youth, and the words of the commendation spoken to his Lord what felt like only yesterday washed over him as he pledged himself to his Lord's son.

"By the Lord, before whom these relics are holy, I will be loyal and true to Leofwine, and love all that he loves, and hate all that he hates, in accordance with God's rights and secular obligations; and never, willingly and intentionally, in word or deed, do anything that is hateful to him; on condition that he keep me as I shall deserve, and carry out all that was our agreement, when I subjected myself to him and chose his favour."

The words dropped like stone in the silent room, but Leofwine grasped his arm, his eyes wild with grief, but also understanding, and something Wulfstan had not expected to see so soon, acceptance and thanks for the task he'd been given.

CHAPTER 12 - AD991

Return to the Battlefield of Maldon

There had been little or no movement on the battlefield since the raiders had left; everything was very much as he'd seen it before he'd left. Vaguely he wondered where they'd gone, and then he realised he didn't care, provided they were gone, and he could recover his Lord's body. It was a cumbersome task, one that he'd far rather not have done, but he knew he owed it to Ælfwine and to his son Leofwine to ensure that he was recovered and buried with all honours.

There were already stray rumours of a poem that had been raised to honour the fallen by the wife of Ealdormen Brythnoth, and Wulfstan wondered if Ælfwine would be mentioned in it? Would Ælfwine fade away from everyone's memories apart from his own, as a dying flame in a summer fire, not needed or heeded until someone remembered that there had been a glow of warmth and that it was now gone? A wisp of remembrance, gone in a moment.

He was not alone as he set to the task of recovering and removing the bodies. Men from the East Anglian fyrd had come to do the terrible work, as had those who'd slunk away from the fight when they'd realised that Ealdorman Brythnoth had miscalculated and that they would die before they won the battle against the raiders.

Wulfstan spoke little, his thoughts introspective and deeply troubled as he wound his way through the corpse field. He didn't do as some did, turn the body over, glance at it and discard it as the incorrect one. No, he along with some of the local men had organised the digging of a large ditch and took all who were recovered to the ditch ready for burial or reclamation. Not everyone would come, and sometimes a decision was made just to bury a body because the wounds were too wicked for any other to look upon; severed limbs, sliced necks, white and gaping open as the body started to disintegrate, even though only two days had passed since the battle.

Wulfstan had spent barely a night at his home. He'd conveyed the unwelcome news of his Lord's death and then he'd reached the conclusion, looking into the startled eyes of his new Lord that he needed to bring his dead Lord home and have him buried in his church lands. Nothing else would be fitting for him. He certainly couldn't leave him to rot away in an abandoned field near the sea.

All through that long night, the dead eyes of Ælfwine had haunted him so that with barely a word to any other, he'd retrieved his horse, and another and had retraced his steps of the day before. This time, he travelled a little more quickly, nervous that by the time he returned some other would have buried his Lord, and he'd never find him.

He'd arrived with a strange relief in the early afternoon heat to spot a few figures winding their way through the dead, and an even greater number of black crows, and the rare four-legged creature worrying at the bodies.

The eyes of the figures had been as hooded as his own, grief straining the faces of young and old alike. A battlefield after the carnage was not a welcoming sight.

Already the communal grave had been constructed, but there was a hesitation in placing the bodies within it, and they proved correct in their persuasions. Throughout the remainder of the day and the long summer night, more and more people had gathered to help with the work, some to loot and steal from the bodies, although little of importance remained. The raiders had been relentless in their search for treasures.

Rumours were flying of where the raiders had gone, and Wulfstan fought down his impulses to leave the battle site and seek out the men responsible for his Lord's death. Neither was he the only one to think it, but caution won out in the end. What good could one man do against five Viking ships loaded with men skilled in the art of warcraft and deceit?

His back ached and twinged from the constant carrying and bending, and it was with a heart grown heavy with grief that he stepped to the next discarded body. This one was staring without seeing at the late sunset, the eyes dull with death. He'd known before he went anywhere near it that it wasn't Ælfwine's body. But he couldn't leave it in its hideous twisted state alone and untended, the right arm trapped under the fallen man, the left leg bent at a horrible angle, and the massive gaping belly wound revealing the dull innards where maggots were already busy at work.

He reached out and closed the man's eyes, aware that he'd briefly seen this man before the battle, cursing himself because he couldn't remember his name. Another man was instantly at the body's feet and without a word, for they'd practised this manoeuvre many times throughout the day, they hefted the ungainly body and began to take it towards the mass grave.

The hum of a prayer reached his ears, and Wulfstan glanced unconsciously to where the local monks had gathered to offer the correct death rites to the bodies. He let the words envelop him and for a brief moment found a respite from his grief and his sorrow in the comforting words of his faith.

The monks stood, like the black crows, around the gaping grave, where the bodies were being tended before burial or retrieval and if they felt the remorse and grief that he did, they were making a good show of masking it. Perhaps they were so caught up in their prayers and songs that the import of what had befallen the Englishmen here had failed to enter their consciousness. He wished he could be as distanced as they were.

Once at the graveside, he gratefully placed the body onto the disturbed earth, wiping sweat from his brow as he did so.

He'd not counted how many bodies he'd moved, but he knew it was too many, and that not one of them had so far been a raider. Had they already claimed their bodies and seen to their death rites? He hoped they had for there'd be little honour in leaving the dead to fend for themselves amongst angry relatives of the fallen. He'd certainly not want to be a member of a war band that had so little regard for dead comrades.

Movement caught his eye, and he glanced up to meet the pinched face of Ælfflaed, Brythnoth's widow. He recognised her from his occasional visits to the Witan. Her clothing was sedate, and a dark cloak enveloped her for all that it was still a warm summer evening. Grief chilled as much as death itself. Sorrow spilt from her body like a wave of fire, and he bowed his head low until she smiled a little at him.

"My thanks for your work here," she murmured, and he wondered if she knew who he was or if she'd spoken to everyone in the same way.

"It was a great slaughter?" she queried again, and Wulfstan felt the need to defend the men who'd met their death.

"The raiders were spineless and took advantage of Brythnoth's greater honour."

Her head swivelled abruptly to look at him, and her gaze was piercing.

"You were here?" she demanded, and he nodded sorrowfully.

"I was yes, my Lord Ælfwine banished me from the battlefield when he knew that the fight was lost. He demanded I return to his son and guide him in his stead."

Her face immediately lost its tense expression, and sympathy entered her eyes.

"You have my compassion for your loss and my thanks for standing with my husband. And I'm pleased to see that of all the men here, you at least were able to do your Lord the honour of carrying out his requests."

Her voice had turned bitter, and he wondered what she'd

heard about the battle and the actions of some of the men.

"I did so unhappily. I would rather have fallen with Ælfwine."

"There is as much honour as dying with your Lord as carrying out his last wishes," and for the first time since Ælfwine had demanded he retire from the battle, Wulfstan felt comforted by his actions.

"I'd not thought of it like that," he admitted, and a tired smile touched his face and the Lady Ælfflaed's.

"Men usually don't," she offered, her gaze fixated on the body at his feet, her face difficult to read.

"My husband acted as he should, you say."

"Yes, he was a perfect commander. He made a rousing speech and we were all committed to ensuring that the raiders went stumbling back to their ships without any success."

"But something went wrong?" she pressed.

"Not wrong exactly. Lord Brythnoth wouldn't fight the raiders who were trapped by the rising tides. He allowed them to touch dry land and sadly, they played a trick on him, and as he patiently waited for them to form up in battle order, a spear pierced him. After that, some refused to fight and retreated without the order to do so having been given."

The news was clearly not what she'd been expecting, and tears filled her eyes.

"He always was a man of too much honour, and I told him until he bored of my conversation that it would mean his death one day."

Wulfstan had no response to give that would give Ælfflaed any solace so he stayed silent, respectfully not watching her as tears dripped from her red-rimmed eyes. He wished he could cry, but tears refused to enter his dry eyes which itched from staring at so much carnage.

She touched his arm as she moved away, whether in thanks or grief or an unconscious attempt to touch a living breathing person amongst so much death he didn't know, but he was grateful for it all the same. It had been a long day, and he had yet to find Ælfwine's body.

Only when the sky was almost black with night did Wulfstan finally stumble upon the body of Ælfwine, and it was the most gruesome discovery of the long, long day. Ælfwine had been stripped naked, his damaged limbs twisted into contorted positions, his head almost severed from his body, and in the dim light, the edges of the damaged skin seemed to pulse with renewed life, but were the maggots already at work on the delicate skin. Thankfully Ælfwine had closed his eyes in death, but Wulfstan was still forced to turn away from the body and heave the contents of his empty stomach onto the blood-streaked grounds.

In the distance, he could hear the crashing of the waves upon the marshy ground and he focused on the noise as he brought his ragged breathing under control and tried to push the crippling grief away from his exhausted limbs.

He'd known full well that when he found Ælfwine, it would be a horrifying experience. After his long day's work, in which he'd almost forgotten his purpose was to find Ælfwine, more intent on the decent burial of the men than on the search for his Lord, he'd told himself that this would be the last body he moved before seeking his bed. Now he wished he'd slept first and then found Ælfwine.

Wiping the bile from his mouth, he stood and cast a resentful look back at the body, rage once more fuelling his actions. How dare the bastards defile the body of his Lord? How dare they strip it of all that marked him as a Lord? If Wulfstan had not made the journey, none would have known that this was the body of a nobleman from Mercia. No, he would have been buried with the rest of the fyrd in a communal grave, and Leofwine would never have had the peace of knowing where his father's corpse lay.

There and then Wulfstan vowed that one day he would have his revenge over the raiders. He would seek out all he could about the men, learn their names, learn about their families, and one day, when they least expected it, he would step into their line of sight and strike their heads from their bodies, and turn their bowels immediately to shit and piss.

Using the anger as leverage to aid his exhausted state, he stood and walked back to Ælfwine. It was almost fully dark now, and he could hear the man who'd been helping him chiding him for still working.

"It is my Lord," he finally managed to choke, and the man instantly stilled his arguments, and instead called to others behind him.

"Bring a torch. This man needs moving tonight."

Wulfstan was unsure how much time passed, but suddenly a bright glow illuminated Ælfwine's still form, and with it, the shadows of grief and anger were pushed away. With determination, Wulfstan stooped and grabbed Ælfwine's shoulders, while his now silent companion grabbed the feet.

The naked body was slippery with damp from the sea, and once or twice, they almost dropped the body, but finally, they reached the place where Wulfstan's two horses had spent the day quietly munching on a farmer's over high hedge line. Delicately, they put the body on the floor so that Wulfstan could remove the cloak and blanket he'd brought to wrap the body within.

The task accomplished, Wulfstan secured the body to the back of the second horse. The horse's eyes looked a little wild and frightened at the load but with words of encouragement, and a gentle nudge from Wulfstan's horse, it stilled and stood silently. Waiting.

Turning to stare once more at the site of the battlefield, Wulfstan extended his hands in thanks to his colleague, and both men clasped arms and then hugged in combined grief.

"My thanks," Wulfstan croaked, and the other man said the same thing at the same time. With a small smile at the strange situation, they found themselves within, Wulfstan took the offered brand once he'd climbed on top of his horse and began his sombre journey home.

He had what he'd come for, and he knew that these other

men would ensure that everyone had a burial. He needed to get Ælfwine home and buried before the corpse decomposed any further.

He kicked his horse to a steady walk, and with the light of the brand, they began their slow way home. He hoped that once his Lord was laid to rest, he'd be able to sleep. He doubted it.

CHAPTER 13 - AD991

Deerhurst

T he service was small and sombre, the young Leofwine barely able to stand, so riddled with grief and remorse. None had been able to speak to him since his father's death, none apart from Wulfstan, and Wulfstan was almost as self-absorbed in his grief as the son. He could admit that with no rancour. He was bereft, and he was angry in equal measure.

Wulfstan and the other men of the household had made all the arrangements with Leofwine's tacit agreement, but really all the boy had done was nod when told to. The brief moment of clarity that Wulfstan had seen when imparting the news had lasted for less time than it took for the story to be known throughout the wooden hall.

Wulfstan had prepared the body for burial himself, alone with his regrets and his loss. He'd not wanted any other to see Ælfwine so broken and bloodied until the young man and friend of Leofwine, Oscetel, had insinuated himself into the proceedings, and Wulfstan had welcomed the assistance. Perhaps, after all, it had been a burden that he needed to share.

"Leofwine's not doing well," Oscetel had whispered as they'd worked. Wulfstan had nodded in understanding.

"It's to be expected. They fought before Ælfwine left."

"I know Wulfstan, but Leofwine needs to stir himself to action. He should be here, not you."

A deep rage had suddenly filled Wulfstan's chest. Why were they discussing the needs of a whining youth when his greatest and oldest friend lay broken and dead before him? He barely contained his ire, pleased that Oscetel chose not to press the matter further. Instead, they worked on in silence, Wulfstan's thoughts returning to the past time and time again, his grief driving his actions.

In the space of that afternoon he replayed the last twenty years of his life, and in doing so discovered he had even more to be sorrowful for than he'd first thought. The son would need to accomplish much if he was to better his father, and in those dark moments of despair and exhaustion, Wulfstan simply didn't think he had the skills or the potential to do so. He cursed his Lord time and time again for allowing himself to be killed, for allowing his son, a youth untried in everything to do with the politics of the Witan to take his place and he railed once more at the actions of the blood thirsty northmen who'd tried their luck on the English coasts. They should have known better. They should have stayed at home. Did they really value treasure above that of their lives?

Before his death, Ælfwine had been adamant, along with Ealdorman Brythnoth, that the King needed to take stronger action against the sporadic attacks of the Norsemen; that they needed to stop them before they became too big to contain with the household troops of the local ealdormen or King's thegn. That the King and his closest advisors hadn't heeded the words added oil to the fire burning inside Wulfstan. The size of the latest raiding army had been monumental when compared with the handful of ships that had previously attacked their land. He'd wondered if the King, grown to manhood in the last few years, would realise that the situation needed handling firmly or whether he'd let others guide his actions as he'd done so while still no more than a boy? It was an interesting predicament.

Now well into his twenties, Wulfstan firmly believed that the

King either needed to enforce his authority or he would forever be little more than a figure head for other people's wants and wishes. The attacks by the raiders would be the perfect way for him to prove himself King and Wulfstan was almost too curious to know how the King would react. It was impossible for the King to ignore the incident that had left Ælfwine and Brythnoth dead. Too many had died at Maldon, one of them a respected ealdorman, and his widow wouldn't let it be for nothing. She was, after all, the King's aunt.

But for now, Wulfstan nursed his grief and glared belligerently at the boy he was supposed to guide to manhood, as the words of the priest washed over him. He was a wreck, unable to sleep, unable to eat and either too lethargic to move or too excitable to sit still.

Wulfstan hoped with time he'd settle, but he was doubtful. The son was an unfinished piece of work, just like King Æthelred. He wondered who would prove to be the wiser man. He didn't hold out much hope for either of them.

CHAPTER 14 –
WINTER AD991

Deerhurst

T he fire was smoky, the wood wet and damp, the summer having turned so quickly to a long and murky winter that everyone had been taken by surprise with their arrangements for the dark time of the year. Some fields had been harvested too late, and the wood, such a vital resource for the fires needed to drive away the chills, had been left outside to absorb the damp. Wulfstan blamed himself for the grim state of his Lord's hall. He shouldn't have let his grief grip him so tightly. He should have held himself against the onslaught of recrimination and crippling anguish.

His young lord sat huddled and miserable before the fire, and Wulfstan felt his heart soften at the grief lines etched into his young face. He was a lost soul who could find comfort in neither God nor friends and with each passing day, Wulfstan watched him sink ever deeper into his angst. It was nothing for him to spend the day and the night before the fire, barely conscious of those around him, and almost oblivious to the frigid conditions.

A few weeks ago a serving girl had hesitantly placed a thick fur around his shoulders when she noticed him shivering. She'd looked uncertain as she'd walked towards him, but Wulfstan having seen the move she'd made and admiring it, had nodded her on when she'd caught his eye. That same cloak still sat around his shoulders and others had followed suit as well. Leofwine resembled a hibernating bear and had the temper to match it.

The entire household was deeply traumatised by the events of the summer, but everyone else was slowly starting to wake from their lethargy. Some of the men had ventured out into the rain soaked fields and cleared the ruined crops knowing that if they didn't the field would be of no use the next year, and others had found and attempted to dry the wood that had been saved for the fire. They'd clearly been less than successful, and Wulfstan would have intervened by now, but he'd heard Oscetel discussing with the others that they needed to pile the wood within one of the small storage barns. Even now, Wulfstan could hear the men calling to each other in the damp air as they carried out that task. They would light a small fire within it, and hopefully, the wood would dry out in the more confined space.

There'd also been a talk of a hunt and Wulfstan thought he might join them. It would be good to feel the steady pounding of the horse's hooves beneath him and to smell fresh air, even if it was festooned with damp. He would like to suggest the same to Leofwine, but the lad heard nothing and focused on less. He ate if food was given to him, and he drank as and when someone remembered that he needed to. Other than that he sat and glared into the fire, not caring that his eyes swam with the smoke of the damp fire, and unheeding of the faint stench of sweat that encircled him.

The lad was a wreck of his former self, and Wulfstan was at a loss as to what to do. He'd never known grief such as this, and he didn't have the skills to draw Leofwine from his gloomy thoughts.

And neither did anyone else.

And the news that slowly filtered through from the Witan was not encouraging either. The King in his wisdom had decided that peace must be made with the raiders. The holiest men and the wisest men of the Witan had decreed that coin would turn the raiders from the shores of England. Wulfstan scoffed at the idea. The men he'd seen weren't just there to be paid off. They'd seen the richness of England's lands, and they'd tasted victory against some of its greatest warriors. The northern men might well take the King's gold, but it was a sign of weakness and Wulfstan knew that the raiders would be back and that they'd interpret it as weakness.

What was needed was a show of strength, a mighty army to meet their ragtag collection of ships and lay bare the hastily thrown together alliances of the men, for not one man had ruled those ships. No, many men had owned the ships, and a few had commanded the men who'd fought at Maldon and those alliances needed to be exploited and exposed for what they were. A façade for bloodthirsty men.

Wulfstan, if he'd had the strength of will, would have told the King precisely that, but he couldn't stir himself to action. Not yet.

The King had sent his condolences to the hall in Deerhurst, but it had been a stranger who delivered the message, and Leofwine had been deaf to it. Wulfstan had tried to be as polite as possible, as accepting as he could be, but he was unhappy with the impersonal response. The King should have come himself, or sent someone from his immediate family. Wulfstan tasted the bile of dishonour whenever he replayed the brief conversation. The King's only concern had been for his own safety, the speech from the messenger had made that clear.

"The King thanks the household for its great sacrifice in keeping his person and the realm secure against the raiders."

Those words played round and round Wulfstan's head, and he knew that soon if he didn't do something with them, they would drive him as half-demented as his wife. And he couldn't let that happen.

A blast of chill air and Wulfstan saw Oscetel poke his head through the door. He caught Wulfstan's eye and nodded. This was it. Make or break.

With a glance towards Leofwine, Wulfstan raised himself carefully to his feet, and half staggered towards the grey and murk of outside.

The stench of damp and fog and horse filled his nostrils immediately, the dull light of outside causing his eyes to fill with tears, they being too accustomed to the candle lit interior of the hall. But as he mounted his horse and breathed deeply of the damp, coughing away the smoke of the fire, he felt a little more alert, a little braver. He could beat his grief. He would do it for his Lord and friend Ælfwine. He only wished he knew how on Earth he could stir Leofwine from his own deep gloom.

CHAPTER 15 –AD992

Deerhurst

T he dark nights lightened and the weather spat and coughed its way to warmth, and still Leofwine did not bestir himself from his place beside the fire pit.

Wulfstan had spent much of the long dark days watching Leofwine with narrowed eyes, pitying him and envying him in equal measure.

Life would have been so much easier if he could only have sunk quite so deeply into the depression that had engulfed his young lord.

No one stirred within the great hall unless it was to cook or to hunt. No one spoke, and no one sang, and certainly no skalds were welcomed to entertain them and shorten the interminable wait for better weather.

The dark winter was a miserable time for everyone, only lessoned by the generous helpings of food and the good strong mead that Ælfwine had liked to serve at his table.

The hall was short of more than just Ælfwine. Only Wulfstan had returned from the handful of men who'd journeyed to Maldon and Leofwine was not alone with his grief. The wives of the seven dead men and their children were gloomy and down hearted. And a little resentful. Wulfstan had brought home only Lord Ælfwine's body. The other men were encased forever in a turf grave far from home and far from their family, near to a belligerent sea that cared not at all about the unwelcome guests it'd transported to the lands of the English.

Not even the words of the Abbot and his monks could lesson the grief and the loss. And Leofwine was no more capable of acting the noble and righteous Lord than he was of feeding himself and cleaning himself.

Wulfstan despaired and sank once more into his own grief, a grief he only wakened from when riding his horse through the crisp landscape of winter.

"Wulfstan," a persistent voice, but not an unwelcome one.

"Oscetel," Wulfstan responded wearily. The young man was not a thorn in his side, but his constant reminders about what he and Leofwine should be doing were starting to wear down Wulfstan's gloomy resolve, and he resented that.

"It's time to rip Leofwine from his grief. The good weather is almost upon us. The time for pain and black times is gone. The men need to train. The seeds need to be sown, and the Lord of this hall needs to be a Lord in more than just name."

Wulfstan agreed with Oscetel's sentiments. He was right. Leofwine had grieved for too long already.

"The girl?" he queried querulously.

"She draws closer to him, but still, not close enough."

Wulfstan sighed in frustration. He'd felt as much. The young servant girl was attractive enough, but Leofwine couldn't see it, too caught up in his own grief, and Wulfstan's hope that his Lord's son would expel his grief through desperate passion was turning to dust, just as his Lord's bones did in their hole in the ground.

"Can't you thrust them together?" Wulfstan asked with exasperation. Surely he didn't need to show the young Lord what to do with a woman?

"I fail to see how, other than having her wait in his bed, but he so little uses it that she could be there a week before he's aware of her."

Wulfstan felt a smile stir his straight face at that. Oscetel was right, again, and his frustration was as funny as the truth of his words.

"I think we should try it," he said, his mouth uttering the words before he'd fully considered them.

Oscetel's face showed his shock before he nodded dutifully and turned to do his duty.

Wulfstan restrained him for a moment with a hand on his shoulder.

"Make sure the girl knows she has a choice. This isn't a command, and I don't want her to think it is one."

Nodding to show he understood, Oscetel caught the girl's eye and beckoned her towards him. She came, but unwillingly, casting looks at Leofwine's back the whole time. Wulfstan worried for a moment that she would be outraged, but as soon as Oscetel began to speak, her tense posture softened, and she nodded and looked back towards Leofwine with longing. Whether Leofwine was aware or not, the girl wanted him. That much was evident.

Wulfstan allowed a smile to curve his mouth again. Perhaps the lovely thing would tempt him if Oscetel gave him enough mead. Her full mouth was welcoming, her long dark hair always gleamed in the firelight, and her clothes, while plain, were always clean and well cared for. Of them all alone, she appeared not to have suffered the depravations of winter and loss combined. Her slight figure curved in all the right place, and Wulfstan couldn't deny that if he'd been a younger man, he too might have found comfort in her embrace if she'd offered it.

Unaware of the plot that was being hatched around him, Leofwine stood and stretched, moving around the hall more than he had in a week. Wulfstan watched with intrigue as Leofwine left the hall, and returned later, his layer of furs discarded, his hair groomed and his beard neatly trimmed, his clothing refreshed. His eyes were still dull, but clearly, his stench had become even too much for him, and he'd forced himself to bathe and see to his body's needs. The girl would perhaps find some pleasure in being with him now.

Oscetel approached Leofwine and spoke a few words before handing him a drinking horn and sitting beside him at the open fire. Leofwine ate and drank, and drank a whole lot more, and finally, as the shutters on the windows flapped in a stiffening wind, and the rain from outdoors could be heard pattering on the roof above, Leofwine allowed himself to be escorted to his bed in a drunken stagger.

As Leofwine entered the room his father had previously used as his own, Wulfstan turned away, a tear of grief combining with one of joy. He hoped that in the morning young Leofwine would have become a man once more, and with it, his lust for power and glory and revenge would have been rekindled.

CHAPTER 16 –
SUMMER AD992

Deerhurst

Wulfstan almost got his wish the following morning when the girl appeared from Leofwine's bedchamber with a smile on her face, and Leofwine appeared a few moments later looking a little sheepish. And yet, in reality, Leofwine's return to the land of the living took much of the following year, so that by the time the anniversary of his father's death had rolled round for the first time, he was almost himself. The servant girl, Hild, quickly became his constant companion both in the bed and out of it, and Wulfstan found he could smile more freely too, now that Leofwine appeared to be coming to terms with his grief.

Wulfstan decided that Leofwine would always wear his sadness too heavily and too openly, but thought that it might make him a wiser man. Men who understood grief made better commanders, better leaders. Wulfstan had always thought so, and Ælfwine had proved the point. Bereaved by his wife's death when his only son was no more than a babe, until the fateful Battle of Maldon he'd never acted without thought for the consequences, not once. Well, maybe just the once, but never again. Not until Maldon, and yet even then, the evidence of Wulfstan's survival was that his Lord, even in that moment of impending doom, was thinking of his son and the survival of his family name.

Wulfstan spent the summer months putting Ælfwine's home back together with the support of Leofwine. He commissioned craftsmen to repair the exterior of the property and set the younger men to shoring up the wicker fences that encased the farm animals and kept them from straying too far.

He also set himself the task of repairing the defences around the house. The river that ran through the back of the farm was a natural deterrent, often deep with floodwater, and criss crossed with deadly currents. The front of the hall was more open, Ælfwine enjoying the relative calm of his life as an adult, and not adding gates or a robust ditch to deter any attackers, even though he'd once said he would. Wulfstan decided that now was the time to add as many defensive features as possible.

The young men of his Lord's household troops, those who last year were deemed too young to fight with their Lord, were set the task of creating and building a ditch and a rampart. It sounded simple enough, but the young men squabbled and fought their way through their differing ideas on how they should proceed.

Wulfstan left them to it. It was an experiment. He wanted to test both Leofwine, and the other men, especially Oscetel. He thought that Leofwine's closest friend and confidant might just have a spark of something special about him. And if he didn't, well, it was better to find that out now.

So Wulfstan arranged that each morning the five youths, now augmented with some older men who'd come to pledge their commendation to Leofwine after the death of his men and his father, trained and learned how to fight in a shield wall, in one to one combat and against a far superior force. And in the afternoons, they learned, or tried to find out how to defend the property and how to work as a team. The mornings were more successful than the afternoons.

As the summer progressed, Leofwine slowly became less a

wavering figure on the periphery of events within the hall, and more an active combatant. He learned to fight viciously and with precision during the training sessions, and his slight figure from the depravations of the winter filled out and allowed him to become even more menacing. He returned to being the warrior his father had trained him to be.

On one particular morning, Leofwine was facing Oscetel, while Leofgar watched on, shouting encouragement and derision in equal part. He wasn't the most skilled warrior that Wulfstan had ever trained, but Leofgar moved with precision and employed a technique that Wulfstan admired. He always outmanoeuvred the others and was excellent at pointing out the weaknesses in both attack and defence.

"Leofwine, you need to keep your shield closer, your sword lower. You're projecting what you're thinking, and that means that Oscetel, for all that he's a bit crap with his sword, beats you every time."

The two boys, used to Leofgar's derisive comments, reacted not at all to being criticised, and in fact, Oscetel offered his friend a grin of delight at being deemed 'crap' with a sword, and Leofwine slyly took advantage of his distraction to deliver a stunning blow to Oscetel's wooden shield. Wulfstan smirked with amusement at Oscetel's annoyed reaction and his outlandish counter move that saw him dancing around Leofwine's back and trying to slice the padded shirt from his back.

Leofwine turned abruptly when he realised what his friend was attempting, and dropping his sword and shield in an untidy heap at his feet, leapt over them both and grabbed his smaller dagger. Oscetel backed away with a wary expression on his face, trying to raise his hands in deference, but in doing so raising his own shield and sword. A look of anger flashed across Leofwine's face, and Wulfstan stood abruptly. He'd not seen so much emotion on the boy's face in nearly a year.

A howl of rage erupted from Leofwine, and Oscetel quickly took refuge behind his shield as Leofwine stalked closer and closer to him.

"You dirty bastard," Leofwine howled as Wulfstan readied himself to intervene in the argument.

"You'd have done the same," Oscetel shouted back, his voice high and showing no fear although he held his shield in front of him. Wulfstan could see where Leofgar was looking a bit uncertain, and he assumed that he was wondering what he'd done to incite such a sudden turn of events. "You did do the same. You took advantage of the fact that I was distracted by Leofgar and you tried to knock me down."

"I didn't try to knock you to the ground from behind," Leofwine roared, and Wulfstan looked at the black expression on Leofwine's face wondering what had caused it.

"I didn't realise you wanted to be a warrior in the ways of the north men?" Leofwine taunted, "taking advantage of people by attacking from behind."

And suddenly it all made a lot more sense.

Leofwine had seen his father's body when it'd been brought back from the battlefield at Maldon, and there was no denying that a sword had impaled his father from behind. Wulfstan had assumed that it must have happened after he was already dead, although he had no proof of that. Apparently, Leofwine had jumped to different conclusions.

Oscetel's face flushed with anger at the intended slight. No one in the household wanted to be named as either a Viking or a Northman, and he stepped towards Leofwine, forgetting his previous wish to end the altercation peacefully.

"I was only trying to show your weaknesses," Oscetel shouted, "like Leofgar's doing when he shouts his insults."

"No, you were trying to make a point, and you were going to make the point that it's better to be a man of no honour when fighting one on one."

Oscetel growled in frustration at the belligerence in Leofwine's voice.

"I was trying to do no such thing, you arse."

Leofwine's already dark face turned to thunder and Wulfstan sighed at the stupidity of the unfolding argument.

"Leofwine," he called, hoping to get his attention, but Leofwine was walking towards Oscetel, his dagger in his hand, and a look of intent on his face.

"Leofwine," he called again, more sharply this time, but still he received no response, and Oscetel was casting him looks of concern the closer Leofwine came. It was evident he'd decided not to make the situation more difficult by threatening Leofwine but neither did he know how to resolve it.

Turning to Wulfhelm, Wulfstan handed his own weapons to the man, including his padded training tunic, and stepped behind the glowering Leofwine, unarmed and unprotected. He reached out and touched Leofwine on the shoulder.

Like a flash of lightning, Leofwine turned to face a new threat, scything his dagger in his hands as he did so. A quick gasp of pain and Wulfstan was holding his face as blood poured from what he hoped was a shallow cut. Leofwine's face showed obvious contrition, but Wulfstan wasn't about to make light of the accident.

Instead, he let his anger billow,

"Leofwine," he shouted, so that everyone working in the yard, be they servant or the blacksmith re-shoeing the horses, turned to see what was happening. Leofwine's face went from contrition to anger in the blink of an eye, and Wulfstan took a step forward so that he was shouting face to face with him, his spittle flying from his lips and landing on Leofwine's young face.

"Oscetel did nothing wrong, and neither is he training to be a Viking raider. And he showed you that while you thought you had the upper hand, he's discovered where you're weak. That's an excellent fighting technique and nothing to be berated for."

Leofwine eyed Wulfstan with his keen eyes, and then they flattened, as they so often had in the past, and Wulfstan hoped he'd not undone the advances of the last half a year.

"He should have submitted."

"That's not what would happen in battle."

"How would you know?" Leofwine screamed in rage, and Wulfstan felt a hollow feeling in his stomach. So this was the problem. Leofwine thought him a coward.

"I know because I've fought against the north men many times in my life, and I understand how they fight. I think you forget boy," and he used the word boy with derision, "that I was the commander of your men's household troops for more years than you've been on this Earth."

"And yet you let him die!"

"I didn't let him 'die'," Wulfstan said knowing that he spoke of his father, "I did what I was commanded to do. I followed his request."

Leofwine's eyes were dark and hooded, and yet grief played at the corners, and Wulfstan thought for a moment that he'd succumb to tears. Instead, he dashed the corners of his eyes and turned to Oscetel.

"Apologies for my actions Oscetel," Leofwine spoke clearly so that all could hear, but clipped. "And Wulfstan, my sincere apologies for your wound." With his voice tight, and a slight bow to both of them, Leofwine took himself inside his hall being careful to leave his weapons at the door and remove his fighting tunic.

Wulfstan watched him with unease and then made a snap decision. He wasn't going to let him get away with that sort of behaviour. Raising his voice he shouted for Leofwine, and before he could draw breath to repeat himself, Leofwine appeared at the door, his eyes quizzical.

"Your apology isn't enough," he said simply as Leofwine bristled with the indignity of being called to order by Wulfstan.

"What would you have me do?" he demanded, and Wulfstan felt the beginning of a plan to ensure that Leofwine learnt how to lead men, not just swear at them.

"You and Oscetel, you'll work on the ditch and complete it, together and without the help of others."

Leofwine looked at Wulfstan with disbelief and Oscetel's shoulders slumped simultaneously.

"Now get on with it," he commanded, surprised when Oscetel and Leofwine both began to walk towards the discarded tools and pick up a heavy shovel each.

"You'll work until sun down, and then I'll assess your progress," Wulfstan shouted, and watched until he could see both men embroiled in the task. Then he turned to Leofgar.

"Keep an eye on them, but don't be too obvious about it. I don't want Leofwine trying to attack Oscetel again."

Leofgar nodded in understanding and positioned himself at the gatepost under construction by the master craftsman to hold half of the gate.

Unconvinced that his scheme would work, Wulfstan nonetheless made himself walk into the hall and leave the two busy at work. He didn't care how long it took, but he would teach Leofwine that he not only could command, but that he would command well.

It took over a week for Leofwine to calm down enough to resolve his differences with Oscetel. Each night of that week, the two lads stomped inside the hall at the end of their long day digging out the new defensive ditch that would surround the hall. They were dirty and smelly and by the second night had learned that if they didn't immediately dunk themselves in the cold river water streaming past the house, no one would speak to them and the smell would be abhorrent, infecting the hall and permeating even the food they were offered.

Wulfstan spent the first few days inside the hall, doing his best to ignore the super heated glares he was the proud recipient of from Leofwine, but by day four, Leofgar had told him it was probably safe enough for him to come outside while the young men worked.

"They're hardly speaking to each other yet," he qualified, "but they're being respectful enough of each other and trying their best to work together."

The news pleased Wulfstan, although it was another two days before Leofwine stopped casting angry and annoyed looks at him.

When he woke on the eighth morning to the sound of laughter coming from the ditch, he smirked a little with delight. He wasn't smug at being proved right. He was quietly pleased that the ploy had worked.

Oscetel and Leofwine needed to be friends who trusted each other as well as being bound by the bond of lordship. Leofwine might not yet be secure in his position at the King's Witan, but Wulfstan could sense the change coming, and he would need people to support on and whom he could rely on. Men other than Wulfstan.

King Æthelred was a confident man now, happy to take charge and make changes where they were needed, and even better, make apologies and reparation where that was necessary. It mostly concerned the church, but Wulfstan didn't care as long as the ripple of unease that had long run through the Witan finally started to ease.

Old, trusted warriors who'd supported the King's father and mother were gone, reduced to death by their ages and Wulfstan hoped something new and good would come in the future. He also firmly believed that Leofwine would be a part of it, just as Ælfwine had wanted to be in the past before his death. The King wanted men to help him rule that had a connection with the places they governed and who understood the people there.

Wulfstan felt a stirring of excitement for the coming years. He'd never thought he'd get over the loss of his friend and the estrangement from his children, but he had, and he was. The future was something to be cherished.

CHAPTER 17 - AD994

The Witan

W ulfstan watched his young Lord with interest, curious to see how he'd manage amongst the hustle and bustle of the Witan if he'd make the same mistakes that his father had once made.

Leofwine was dressed well, but not too well. He carried himself with a casual grace that hid the nerves that had kept him up all night. His young face somehow absorbed his lack of sleep, while Wulfstan knew his face was greyed with fatigue. He hoped the day would pass quickly, but knew from experience that it wouldn't. Æthelred, a man, grown to maturity under his own eyes, had created an image of himself that relied wholly on protocol and ceremony. The day would be long and dull, the feast that night would be the first opportunity to relax.

The palace was richly decorated and as Wulfstan walked inside he almost missed his step when he saw the King's mother already seated on the side of the hall reserved for the King's family. It wasn't that she'd disappeared from all formal events in the last few years, but she'd been forgotten about at the back of the hall. Wulfstan wondered why she was back? He'd heard nothing throughout the winter months to hint at a reconciliation between the King and his mother that would make her once more part of the select few who governed the land.

He wondered if the King's impending alliance with the Viking hoard whom they'd faced at Maldon and who'd returned the previous summer had forced him to rely on her once more. She'd always been a voice of reason amongst the men who held more power than the women. Wulfstan watched her pensively.

She'd aged, that was certain, but her eyes had remained bright and her hair lustrous. He could almost blink and be back fifteen years ago. Her eyes swept those coming into the hall, and he could have sworn that they lingered on him for a moment too long, a faint smile on her lips.

He wondered what she saw when she looked at him? Did she notice the grey hair and grey beard? The tired eyes and the lines etched onto his face or did she see him as he'd once been?

In front of him, Leofwine was making his way to the front of the assembly, speaking to those he knew as he went, shaking the hands of others who were keen to meet their new ealdorman. Not that he was alone in his appointment. No, a series of deaths had finally robbed the King of all but Ealdorman Æthelweard from the beginning of his reign, and he'd been forced to appoint new men to fill the voids in the east of ancient Mercia and the lands of the East Saxons. Leofsige would join Leofwine when he went before his King and pledged himself as his commended man. Only the year before Ælfhelm had been appointed to the suddenly vacant Northumbrian ealdormany. Where before there'd been three ealdormen there would soon be five, and the King needed them.

Wulfstan watched Ælfhelm with curiosity. He was an unknown to Wulfstan, and his position had been gained after the disgraced Thored, father in law to the King, had been deprived of his ealdormany and sent into exile. Wulfstan suddenly realised that was probably why the King's mother was back and on prominent display. His adopted family had failed the King, and now he needed to resort to his birth family.

The King arrived in the midst of Wulfstan's musings, and his eyes turned warmly to greet Leofwine. While their initial meeting had been awkward, Leofwine's time in the King's household before his father's death had allowed them to forge a closer friendship. Wulfstan didn't think it was necessarily a healthy friendship yet, but he had high hopes for Leofwine. He was a thoughtful young man, someone the King would do well to bring into his close counsel and more importantly, trust. The King apparently thought the same, and although his appointment as Ealdorman brought with it new obligations and the knowledge that he'd been leaving England for Norway shortly, to act on the King's behalf, it also had some more attractive incentives.

Despite his worry that the day would drag, the business of the Witan was concluded quickly, and Wulfstan grinned with pride to see his young Lord become an ealdorman. He spared a thought for his missing friend, Ælfwine, a brief sadness squeezing his heart, but he managed to turn the thoughts to those of happiness soon enough. Ælfwine would have been overjoyed to see his son holding his own amongst the men of the Witan and he'd certainly done better than Ælfwine's own disastrous first appearance. Not that he'd be telling Leofwine as such, and Wulfstan realised, Leofwine had spent more time around the Witan than Ælfwine ever had. He was far better prepared than his father had ever been but some things they never spoke about, just like the battle that had killed his father.

Leofwine managed to make his way to Wulfstan through the crowd of well-wishers and reached out to clasp his arm in joy. The grin on his face was threatening to overflow down his neck and onto his shoulders and Wulfstan found it infectious, his face mirroring that of Leofwine's.

He leant forward and whispered congratulations to Leofwine.

"You spoke clearly and well."

"Good, I was sure I'd trip over my tongue when I made my commendatory oath."

Wulfstan joined in his delighted laughter then, only noticing that King Æthelred had joined them when there was a hush in the conversation around them.

"Ealdorman Leofwine," Æthelred said, rolling his tongue around the word with relish. "I have someone I want to introduce you to."

"My Lord," Leofwine responded, all trace of humour gone from his voice, the ealdorman once more.

"This is Æthelflaed," and from beside Æthelred, a young woman stepped forward, a faint flush on her face and the same on Leofwine's own.

"My Lady Æthelflaed," Leofwine said reaching out to take her hand in a gentle clasp of friendship. She met his gaze demurely, and Wulfstan suppressed a chuckle of amusement, his eyes meeting Æthelred's, as the couple officially met for the first time. Leofwine knew that the King was planning on arranging a marriage for him but Wulfstan doubted he'd realised how beautiful his future wife was going to be.

Æthelred spoke above them both.

"You should become acquainted with each other, and if you decide you'll be compatible, we can arrange the wedding as soon as possible." With a small smile on his face, he moved away from the couple, leaving Wulfstan to supervise them both.

Wulfstan glanced at the girl appraisingly. He'd heard of her but had never seen her close enough to realise that she was beautiful. Her hair was long and lustrous, the deep brown cascading down her shoulders and her eyes were piercingly green. She was dressed in a soft dress of blue cloth, embellished with small jewels and with highly polished brooches at the shoulder.

Besides the girl, an older woman hovered, and Wulfstan gazed at her. Was she Æthelflaed's mother? He opened his mouth to speak, but the woman pursed her lips and turned slightly to the side, making it clear that she had no intention of talking to him. Wulfstan felt his anger stir a little. If the King thought the girl good enough for Leofwine, then the mother had nothing to worry about. After all, he was now an ealdorman, a good match for any young woman.

"My Lady," he said stepping towards her, his mouth set in just as much of a stubborn line as her own.

"Wulfstan," she responded coldly, and Wulfstan suppressed a smirk of amusement. She'd clearly decided to be unpleasant, and that just enticed Wulfstan to be beyond polite and pleasant.

"Your daughter is pleased with the match?" he asked, turning slightly so that the older woman, more of an age with himself, could not gaze quite so spitefully at the young pair.

"It doesn't matter whether she is or not. It will go ahead."

"Ealdorman Leofwine," and he ensured he stressed the word Ealdorman, "is a firm favourite of the King. I hope she'll be pleased to know she has the ear of the King."

"Hum," the woman responded, and Wulfstan heard every reservation there was behind that single sound. He was not blind to the unease that currently infected the people of England. The attack three years ago, so monumental and devastating, coming as it did after a decade that had seen little more than the odd shipload of Vikings trying their luck around the English coastline, had worried people. The payment of the large geld, the death of Ealdorman Brythnoth and the treachery of Ealdorman Ælfric and the disappearance from public view of Ealdorman Thored, father of the King's wife, had unnerved people. Now that Olaf and his men were back that unease had intensified.

The acknowledgement that a further geld would be paid, that Olaf would be baptised with King Æthelred as his godfather and the knowledge that Leofwine would shortly be escorting Olaf back to his homeland of Norway was not proving to be quite as successful as the King might have hoped.

Wulfstan had been surprised and dismayed by the payment of the geld after the disaster at Maldon, but he'd reconciled himself to it. Better to lose money that the kingdom had in abundance than men who could never be replaced. Now that Olaf was back once more, and rumour had it with the son of the King of Denmark as his ally, Wulfstan was more circumspect. He wanted the geld to work, he wanted Leofwine to prove himself as a competent ambassador for the King but, Swein of Denmark. He worried him far more than Olaf ever had, despite his hand in the death of Ælfwine.

That knowledge about Olaf had cost Wulfstan dearly when Leofwine had discussed it with him. The two men had never spoken about Olaf's place in the death of Ælfwine. Olaf might have led the raid, been paid to go away, but Leofwine had managed to remain ignorant of that one salient fact. When Æthelred ordered Leofwine to journey with Olaf, Wulfstan had felt a deep feeling of foreboding. The father was bad enough, but there was no way that Olaf would murder the son as well. He'd never allow it.

Somehow he'd managed to keep his thoughts to himself and ensure that he accompanied Leofwine on his sea voyage. Not that the thought settled him. He'd never been a man who enjoyed the swell of the sea, and he knew he'd be sick and ill on the journey, but at least he would be there, as would an entire shipload of men loyal to the King and by default, Æthelred.

He was pulled from his thoughts by Leofwine grabbing his arm, if possible his grin even wider than it had been before.

"She's delightful and beautiful," he gushed, his eyes never leaving the retreating back of the young woman as she walked away, her mother speaking urgently into her ear as she did.

"Pity the mother isn't," Wulfstan offered sourly but Leofwine was too caught up to in his excitement to heed his words.

"We will spend time together tomorrow, and then, if we both agree and I've asked her to be very honest with the King, we'll arrange to wed as soon as we can. How long before the baptism?" he asked in a rush of words, and Wulfstan rolled his eyes at the exuberance of the lad.

"Not until September," he said, "there's time enough for the pair of you to take your time and consider if it's what you want."

"Oh I want it," Leofwine said, chuckling as he did so. Wulfstan rolled his eyes once more and turned to see Oscetel at his side.

"Can you speak sense to him?" the older man asked, but Oscetel was as bewitched by the woman as Leofwine.

"Oh to be young and only think with your dick," Wulfstan finally muttered, earning himself a shocked expression from both the young lads.

"You disagree?" he asked with a smirk, turning to leave the church.

"Wulfstan, I think only of politics," Leofwine called as he left, his voice outraged and amused at the same time.

"Of course you do," Wulfstan said sourly, before finding himself in the gentle afternoon sunshine once more.

Leofwine was an ealdorman; he would soon have a wife and his own children. Wulfstan wondered just how much longer his Lord's son would want to keep him around for. He had his advisors and warriors ready to lead the household troops, and yet Wulfstan felt a prickle of unease.

Olaf.

He wasn't happy that Olaf was to be Leofwine's first project as ealdorman.

A week later, much to Wulfstan's amusement, Leofwine and Æthelflaed were married before the King, both blushing in equal measure. It was clear that Leofwine was pleased with the match. Wulfstan had already decided that it would be best if the girl were as distanced as possible from her less than impressed parents. They might strengthen Leofwine's ties to the ancient Hwiccan province of Mercia, but it was the family name that seemed to matter, not the people themselves. They appeared to be incapable of saying anything positive, and Wulfstan wondered how they'd managed to produce a daughter who was so beguiling.

With the wedding completed, Leofwine turned his attention to his rapidly approaching sea journey. The King had already told him that he would be gifted with a ship worthy of his position for the journey but when it was finally unveiled even Wulfstan was amazed by the beauty of the ship.

At his side, Leofwine had whistled in amazement, and Æthelred had smirked with delight.

"She was given to me by Ealdorman Æthelweard, and now I give her to you. She's no more than ten years old and was built by the finest craftsmen that Æthelweard could find and afford. Her crew has been together for most of that time, and Æthelweard has warned me repeatedly, that her captain, Ælfric, is a man not to be crossed or trifled with. He thinks only of his ship and will have no concern for your comfort or your worries."

Wulfstan chuckled at the description of the man he'd spied earlier in the day, haranguing his crew to ensure she shone as though a summer's day burst through her well-tempered hull. If Leofwine had to travel across the sea, and if Wulfstan had to go with him, he felt slightly mollified that the King at least appreciated the sacrifice and the peril they were placing themselves within.

The King didn't allow Leofwine long to examine his ship in detail.

"We need to have a final conversation about your contact with Olaf. I've met the man, and I find him to be quite interesting. I'm confident that this time, he will keep to his agreement to stay away from English shores. But whenever you get the opportunity I want you to discuss how poor England now is in the wake of the geld, and I want you to make sure he realises that next time there will be no money, only the bloody end of a sword embedded in his bowels."

Leofwine was serious as he listened and Wulfstan felt his eyebrows rise in shock at the King's tone. In the past, he'd been the last to agree to any form of violence as retaliation, apparently, Olaf's return to England had angered him. Wulfstan understood that the King planned to call for his ealdormen to employ more household troops and train the fyrd better so that any recurrence of violence could be put down far sooner and without the recourse to a geld payment.

Wulfstan wasn't sure his plans would ever come to fruition, but then, the King had surprised him before.

"You'll be at the baptism as will the Archbishop and myself. After that, the geld will be paid, and Olaf will be escorted from English land. Aim him towards the land of the Scots and make sure he keeps on going. And don't let him rattle you. He's a confident man and his confidence needs turning towards Norway. Tell him he'll be a great King, a most Christian King, but only if he stays in Norway and leaves England alone."

Leofwine was nodding as he listened to his King. They'd discussed this at length in the Witan after he'd been made an ealdorman, and it was clear that the King trusted him to act in his best interests. Well, it was either that or he'd decided that Leofwine was the most disposable of them all. Wulfstan hoped that wasn't at the heart of Æthelred's decisions, but, well sometimes when he slept, he woke in a panic convinced that despite Æthelred's honeyed words, he meant Leofwine ill. Perhaps, after all, he remembered their first unfortunate meeting and his father's ill-advised proposal to his mother and had waited for all these years to punish him.

Wulfstan hoped he was wrong, but he couldn't entirely banish his worry.

CHAPTER 18 – AD995

The Coast

T he jovial voice of Olaf woke Wulfstan from his disturbed night's sleep. He gazed into the grey light of dawn and suppressed a groan. Damn the man. Did he never sleep? They'd been up long past any reasonable time to seek their bed, drinking and singing, and now he woke them all before the sun had even risen and was shouting for the men to be in their ships and away.

He almost thought the man was nervous to be gone, but that went against everything he knew about him. No, he thought that Olaf was solely driven by his need to be home, back where he felt he belonged. He'd been a wanderer for much of his life.

Beside him, Leofwine groaned loudly, and Wulfstan smirked. Leofwine had drunk far more last night than was good for a young man on his first sea voyage. There was some consolation in knowing that Leofwine would suffer more than he would.

"Come my Lord you should be about and on your feet."

"Ah sod off Wulfstan," Leofwine moaned but that only made Wulfstan laugh out loud.

"You should learn when to stop."

"I can't stop until Olaf does, and you know it."

"Olaf is a man twice your age, who knows how to drink and how to fight. You know how to fight."

"You never taught me to drink," Leofwine muttered angrily as he sat up, rubbing grit from his eyes and holding his head.

"Drinking the night away isn't how young Lord's should spend their time."

"That might be true, but when Vikings ask you to, you have to say yes."

"Didn't you think about pretending?" Wulfstan asked, intrigued now. He'd always thought that Leofwine was intelligent. He was surprised he'd drunk so much.

'Why should I pretend? I'm to make friends with Olaf, show him that the English can be his allies more than his enemy."

"Well, all you did last night was prove that an Englishman can make a real fool of himself when he can't hold his drink."

Leofwine flashed him a look of annoyance but then relented.

"You might well have a point. Did I do anything too embarrassing?"

"Not as I recall. You fell asleep too soon."

"Ah," Leofwine groaned, staggering to his feet and taking the drinking bottle from Wulfstan gratefully. He swigged as much water as he could, as quickly as he could and then passed the bottle back to Wulfstan.

"How much did you drink?" he asked, offering his hand to Wulfstan, who staggered to his feet as well. He was pleased to see that he was steadier on his feet than Leofwine was.

He stretched his back. Sleeping on the floor was the remit of young men, not old ones. They'd only been on their trip for a handful of days, and already he wanted to be home again, back in his comfortable bed.

In the distance, they could see Olaf and his shipmen making their way to their own ships, and Ælfric, their own shipman, was standing, tapping his feet and casting meaningful looks their way.

"Come on Leofwine," Wulfstan said, "let's not upset the old man any more than we already have." He ignored the question about how much he'd had to drink. There was no need to tell the lad he'd drunk very little. He needed to learn that lesson himself.

It was no secret that neither of them was good on the sea, neither was it a secret that Ælfric was an impatient man. When the King had warned Wulfstan that the ship's captain thought only of his ship, he'd not been wrong. The men who worked the oars were used to Ælfric's ways, Wulfstan and Leofwine were not, and they had to jump to attention like small children before a parent. It was almost an amusing situation to be in.

They ate on the ship, Olaf and his men already rowing out to deeper waters. The swell of the waves hit the ship, much to Wulfstan's dismay. He'd thought it was a quiet day and that the sea would be gentle on his stomach. At the front of the ship, Leofwine was struggling even further, and his retching was making all the men exchange knowing looks. None of them had drunk as much as him the night before. They'd all been sleeping after their day's exertion. Wulfstan doubted the lad would be drinking as much again.

Thank goodness.

They still sailed within sight of land, but Wulfstan knew that the time was coming when they'd have to sail out of sight and make their way to the islands to the far north of the land of the Scots. He wasn't looking forward to it, and he'd been thinking hard about how to ensure their safety on the journey. He liked Olaf, but that was a long way from trusting him and once more, his uncertainties about the King's intentions towards Leofwine were plaguing him.

What if the King had decided that Leofwine was expendable? What if Olaf had decided the same? What if he wasn't supposed to return?

They sailed as part of a large force, and the majority of the men owed their allegiance to Olaf, not to Leofwine and the raiders, Viking warriors one and all, had been derisive about Leofwine's sea legs while admiring his ship with lustful eyes. Ælfric had demanded that all the men remain armed at all times, on all the ships under Leofwine's command, but Wulfstan knew that something drastic was needed and he feared that

Leofwine had already made his mind up about the whole thing.

The day passed in an agony of aching heads and heaving stomachs, and he didn't know who was the most relieved to put their feet on dry land as the sun was starting to set, he or Leofwine. Then he reconsidered. It was Leofwine. He might have recovered from his excessive drinking the night before, but the sea voyage, even as uneventful as it had been, had caused his face to turn a deep shade of green.

"How many more days?" he whispered to Wulfstan when they were around the campfire that night.

"We still have a long way to go Leofwine. It'll be as far again; I'm sure of it." Leofwine groaned dramatically, and Wulfstan watched him with shared sympathy.

Olaf chose that moment to weave his way through the sleeping bodies of some of the men and sit before the campfire.

"My Lord Leofwine, tomorrow we'll strike out for the islands known as the Shetlands. It should take two days, no more, and from there, well, it'll be no more than another seven to Norway itself."

"The weather is good for a long sea voyage?" Leofwine asked, the faint hope in his voice difficult to miss.

"Oh yes my Lord Leofwine. The weather will hold. It is perhaps a little too still, and a storm is coming, but it's better to go and face the wrath of the sea than stay here and wait for an invitation from her."

"I see," Leofwine responded, squeezing his eyes tightly shut as he thought of the days and nights he'd need to stay on board the ship.

"It'll go quickly, Lord Leofwine, don't worry. A few days on the open sea and you'll find yourself a natural in a ship. My men and I, we've been in and out of ships since we were mere babes. We can't imagine not knowing how to stand against the deep swells, and we couldn't even for a moment entertain the idea of feeling sick."

Leofwine nodded in understanding, but it was evident he didn't believe Olaf, not for a time being.

"My Lord Olaf," he said, as though an afterthought. "Do you think that perhaps I could be a passenger on your ship for the next few days? It would give us the opportunity to become firmer friends."

Olaf, his eyes narrowing as he heard Leofwine's words and realising the true intent behind them, was already nodding his head in agreement before Leofwine finished speaking.

"Of course Lord Leofwine. I'd be pleased to have you on board my ship. Only by travelling within her can you truly appreciate what a thing of beauty she is. Be ready in the morning as soon as the sun rises. We'll need to make the best use of the light we have."

Without another word, Olaf walked back towards his own men and Leofwine turned to Wulfstan.

"Did I insult him?" he asked with worry. Wulfstan shook his head.

"No, I think he prefers men who speak their mind."

"I hope I'm not as sick on his ship as I am on my own. I don't want the men to have too much to ridicule me for," Leofwine said sourly.

"I don't think the ship will make any difference. You just don't like the sea."

"No, it doesn't agree with me. Not at all."

"Do you think it's wise to travel with Olaf?"

"I don't see that I have any choice. We need to make him stay with our ship. We need to make sure that we do what the King asked us to do."

"Even if it puts you in danger?" Wulfstan pressed. He was concerned that Leofwine wasn't considering all the consequences of what he was being asked to do.

Leofwine turned understanding eyes on Wulfstan.

"I won't blame you if something goes wrong. It's my choice. The King might think he demanded this of me, but he didn't. I agreed to it."

"Olaf," Wulfstan swallowed thickly around the word, "he can't be trusted either."

Leofwine glanced at Wulfstan and fixed him with a sharp look. He knew, but he never asked, and Wulfstan was relieved.

"Olaf, well Olaf. I appreciate your concerns. He's a beguiling man. I can see why so many follow him, and I've not seen him in battle."

Wulfstan nodded as he absorbed the words from his young Lord. He didn't want to tell him what to do. He'd never tried to tell him what to do. He only hoped that he knew what he was doing. Sometimes he didn't see an ealdorman before him, but instead the young lad he'd watched grow to manhood. The years had sped by, far too quickly for Wulfstan's liking and apart from a few moments of uncertainty, he hoped he'd guided the lad well. His desire to put himself in such a precarious position was proof enough that as much as Wulfstan always wanted to play it safe, Leofwine knew enough to know that it wasn't always possible.

"There are five ealdormen, and I'm the youngest of them all. I know the King thinks me expendable, I'd be a fool not to, but Olaf doesn't know that. He thinks it's in his best interests to keep me safe."

Wulfstan considered the words carefully.

"You have a good point. You've thought about it. I'll watch you as much as I can from the ship, but if Olaf makes a run for it, you might find yourself alone."

"I'll have my weapons, if the worst should happen, don't follow me. Go back to England. Support Æthelflaed and my own child, if I'm lucky enough that she's pregnant."

Wulfstan looked hard at Leofwine, wondering if he actually understood the words he was saying. Solemn eyes looked back his way, and Wulfstan nodded, satisfied. Perhaps, after all, he'd trained Leofwine too well in the duties of a Lord and a representative of the King.

EPILOGUE - AD1012

The cry of the child jarred him from his deep sleep, and he smiled with delight. Lord Leofwine was a grandfather. It wouldn't please Leofwine, Wulfstan thought wryly, but it pleased Wulfstan. Northman would be a kind and caring father. The mother seemed a tender soul. The child was lucky to have such parents.

His back was stiff, his neck almost too painful to move and he knew that his breaths were numbered. He'd felt it all night. The hand of death squeezing a little tighter with each laboured breath, but he'd fought it, wanting to know that the child was safely born before he let death take him.

The fire was warm before his covered knees, and the fur pulled tightly around him. Æthelflaed's work before she'd retired for the night, or been woken in the early dawn to help her son and his new wife. She would be a doting grandmother, and Wulfstan thought afresh what a pity it was that she'd have no more children herself.

This family of his Lord's had been more than his own to him. He loved his own children, and now their children. He was proud of their accomplishments, but they were so different to him, men of the land by choice, never happier than when their cows birthed or their crops grew to fruition. He envied them the simple joys and pleasures they'd had. Despite the unhappiness of his marriage and his wife's strange ways, his sons were good men. The sort of men he'd fought for throughout his life;

his shield and sword used to protect them.

To live a life so close to the land, to know what every burst of wind portends, to know which soils would allow the crops to grow, the sheep to fatten and the cows to produce fine milk and healthy calves. They'd been blessed, and he'd made his peace with them. Their children would benefit from his close links with the Ealdorman of the Hwicce and like their fathers, they'd choose how they wanted to live, they could be farmers or warriors. They'd have the choice and support of their local ealdorman. He could ask for nothing more.

But Northman, Leofric, Ealdgyth, Godwine and Eadwine were almost a part of him, and he was sorry he'd see no more of them. He'd enjoyed being there to watch them grow and every extra day that he'd had, since that fateful day when Leofwine's father had sent him home to watch his son, had been a bonus, a day to enjoy and embrace, and he thanked his God for that.

He was no longer sorry he'd ridden away from the battlefield that day and left his Lord to die. His Lord's honour earned on that long ago day, nearly a quarter of a century ago, had made his son a man of renown, a man of power and grace; a man to be close to and be honoured to call a friend, a Lord or even an enemy. He'd had the ear of a King or two in his time, the enmity of another King, the love of his wife and the respect of the King's wife. He'd basked in Leofwine's accomplishments, and bled with him too when he was wounded or injured, or beaten down by the stress of his position.

He'd miss him most of all, the young child, grown to maturity and beyond before his very eyes. Leofwine, a man his father would have been proud of and amazed in equal measure.

He'd miss Wulfstan too. Wulfstan feared the impact his death would have on him, but he could do nothing more for him now. His time had come to pass. He was old and stooped and past his prime, forgetting more than he remembered, and sometimes smelling none too good either. Not that Leofwine would ever say anything, or Æthelflaed, and certainly not the servant who tended to his every need. He was calm and had gentle hands to help him, and a steady back to support him when he stood. He hoped Leofwine rewarded him for his tenderness towards him.

Before the fire, one of the hounds lifted his head and looked at him. The dog's eyes were as rheumy as Wulfstan's, and he shared a look of sympathy with the old man before him. He'd served his Lord for many, many long years and now he looked for his death as well. So many pups surrounded him that Wulfstan wondered how he coped with them all.

The hound stood stiffly and stretched out the kinks in his back legs, never taking his eyes from Wulfstan. The hound knew what was about to happen as his eyes looked behind Wulfstan. The dog could see the old man's death stalking him.

He placed his muzzle in his weak hand, shaky now and unable to hold anything firmly. His breath was hot in Wulfstan's hand. The hound had time yet and apparently knew it.

Hammer had been almost as much a friend to Wulfstan as Leofwine had, always knowing when he should turn traitor to his master, sharing his worries and his fears. Wulfstan hoped he'd know to go to Oscetel now.

Leofwine inspired such loyalty in man and beast both that Wulfstan sometimes wondered if he knew the effect he had on those who surrounded him. They would all, boy, man and beast, lay down their life for him. He was a lucky man to inspire such total devotion.

"There boy," Wulfstan croaked, his voice catching with disuse. "I see you're a grandfather too," He smirked as he heard the cry of the babe again. He wondered if it was a boy or a girl but he'd never know.

Hammer licked his hand with his roughened tongue as Wulfstan touched his head and his intelligent ears one last time. Hammer honoured him with his presence as his death approached.

The hound settled beside him, his head against his thigh and as his body heat warmed the old man's frigid limb and chilled body, his eyes closed and he knew they'd never open again.

His time was done.

AUTHOR NOTES

Wow, this one has been a nightmare! I thought writing about Wulfstan would be far, far easier than it actually was. I blame myself for trying to go back to the beginning of King Æthelred II's reign, a time of great complexity and over-powerful Ealdormen. I hope I've done him justice and offered my readers some new information and managed to explain his motivations. He's the first official fictitious character I've written about in an historical setting, and I hope that doesn't disappoint too many people to know that he didn't exist.

I've purposefully stopped from retelling the events of Viking Sword, Viking Enemy and Northman Part 1 from Wulfstan's point of view, but it doesn't mean that I won't return to him in the future.

Apologies for the swathe of A names – Ælfwine, Ælfhere, Ælfric, Æthelred. There must have been a reason for it and I'd appreciate it if someone could tell me why?

The more I write about Anglo-Saxon England, the more complex and compelling it becomes and the more stories I want to tell. I'm so pleased that I have the whole swathe of over six hundred years to work with and I have many, many more projects I hope to bring to life in the years to come.

The salient events of the time did happen – Edward was murdered in 978. The Anglo Saxon Chronicle states that he was 'killed' and says nothing else, the rumours about the King's mother only appear later. For more information there's a book devoted to Elfrida which might be worth having a look at. Æthelred did become King when he was a boy. There were sporadic Viking attacks on Southampton, Watchet and Portland and the great ealdormen of the King's father's reign do appear to have continued to play out their arguments about religious reform and land. I've not gone into great detail about it in the novel as I think I need to do some more research.

CAST OF CHARACTERS

Wulfstan (Ælfwine's commended man) fictional (commendatory lordship is a term explained by Baxter in his account of the lives of The Earls of Mercia – it seems to me to be similar to a feudal oath but different all at the same time – the words of the oath are also Baxter's translation.)

Wulflæd (Wulfstan's wife) fictional

Wulf and Wulfhelm (Wulfstan's sons) fictional

At Deerhurst

Ælfwine (of Deerhurst) factual character about whom very little is known. His home in Deerhurst is an educated guess from research on Domesday Book and the lands his descendants owned when the survey was conducted.

Leofwine (Ælfwine's son) factual character

Oscetel (Leofwine's friend) fictional

Ælfnoth, Leofgar and Brithelm (Ælfwine's men) fictional

Heard (Ælfwine's horse) fictional

King Æthelred II (King of England from 978 (about ten years old) factual character

Lady Elfrida (mother of King Æthelred II) factual character

Ælfgifu (Æthelred's wife form about 985) factual character

Ealdorman Thored (Ælfgifu's father and so Æthelred II's father in law)

Ealdorman Ælfhere (of Mercia) factual character

His brother Ealdorman Ælfheah dies before the story begins.

Ealdorman Æthelwine factual character

Ealdorman Brythnoth (of East Anglia) factual character – dies at Battle of Maldon in 991 and immortalized in the Battle of Maldon poem

Ealdorman Æthelweard (of Western Provinces) factual character – wrote a Latin version of Anglo Saxon Chronicle which survives to this day

Ealdorman Ælfric (of Mercia) factual character

King Hywel of Gwynedd (grandson of King Idwal who appears in Brunanburh – if you've read it) factual character

King Einion of Dyfed (grandson of King Hywel Dda who appears in Brunanburh) factual character

Einar – Viking at Portland (fictional)
Eadwig – at Portland (fictional)
Waltheof – at Portland (fictional)
Frithuric – at Portland (fictional)

Places

There is, believe it or not, little consensus about the names of the countries that we now take for granted. When Wales became Wales, when England became England are hotly contested subjects.

As a writer who wants to portray the past as it really was, it's almost a minefield. The term Welsh is an Anglo-Saxon name for 'foreign' so I try to use British or Briton instead, as after all, Wales was the land of the Ancient Britons, but it was divided into kingdoms, as England had been until only recently. The kingdoms of Gwynedd, Dyfed, Powys etc, were just like England, never destined to be united and at this time, there had been the odd King strong enough to unite Wales (see I'm doing it now) but the alliances were based on the power of the men, just as 'England' was formed by Athelstan and had to be reformed under his brother, and for another couple of decades yet.

The ancient Anglo-Saxon Kingdoms of Mercia, Wessex, East Anglia and Northumbria are handy 'handles' but it's not known how much people considered themselves to be one or the other, and of course, even these kingdoms are a combination of many far tinier kingdoms/chieftains, such as the land of the Hwicce, the Magonsaete and others.

MEET THE AUTHOR

I'm an author of fantasy (viking age/dragon themed) and historical fiction (Anglo-Saxon, Vikings and the British Isles as a whole before the Norman Conquest), born in the old Mercian kingdom at some point since the end of Anglo-Saxon England. I write A LOT. You've been warned! Find me at https://mjporterauthor.com and @coloursofunison on twitter.

Books by M J Porter (in series reading order)

Gods and Kings Series (seventh century Britain)
Pagan Warrior
Pagan King
Warrior King

The Ninth Century
The Last King
The Last Warrior
The Last Horse

The Tenth Century

The Lady of Mercia's Daughter

A Conspiracy of Kings

Kingmaker

The King's Daughters

M J PORTER

<u>Chronicles of the English (tenth century Britain)</u>
Brunanburh
Of Kings and Half-Kings
The Second English King

<u>The Mercian Brexit (can be read as a prequel to The First Queen of England)</u>

<u>The First Queen of England (can be read as a prequel to The Earls of Mercia)</u>
The First Queen of England Part 2
The First Queen of England Part 3

<u>The King's Mother</u> (can be read as a sequel to The First Queen, or a prequel to The Earls of Mercia)

Queen Dowager

Once A Queen

<u>The Earls of Mercia</u>
The Earl of Mercia's Father
The Danish King's Enemy
Swein: The Danish King (side story)
Northman Part 1
Northman Part 2
Cnut: The Conqueror (full length side story)
Wulfstan: An Anglo-Saxon Thegn (side story)
The King's Earl
The Earl of Mercia
The English Earl
The Earl's King
Viking King
The English King (coming soon)

<u>The Dragon of Unison (fantasy based on Viking Age Iceland)</u>
Hidden Dragon

166

Dragon Gone
Dragon Alone
Dragon Ally
Dragon Lost
Dragon Bond

Throne of Ash (coming soon)

As JE Porter

The Innkeeper

Made in United States
North Haven, CT
17 September 2023

41675630R10095